T0193896

Sphere Talamh

SPHERE TALAMH

WARP IN TIME...

CRYSTAL CLARY

authorHOUSE®

AuthorHouse™
1663 Liberty Drive
Bloomington, IN 47403
www.authorhouse.com
Phone: 1 (800) 839-8640

Published by AuthorHouse   08/28/2015

ISBN: 978-1-5049-3432-9 (sc)
ISBN: 978-1-5049-3433-6 (hc)
ISBN: 978-1-5049-3431-2 (e)

Library of Congress Control Number: 2015914036

Print information available on the last page.

Artwork by William Daun

This book is printed on acid-free paper.

DEDICATION

A special thank you to my husband and son for all of your enthusiasm and support.

To my father for being such an inspiration to follow.

Lastly, thank you, Mom and Nana, for always being such an important part of my life.

PROLOGUE

WARP IN TIME ...

Chapter 1

THE SPHERE

RICHARD CLARY BEARS A SOLEMN appearance on his face. He begins to pace the circumference of the crash site. Broken pieces of metal and a coil surround the crashed object. Fire is still flaring out from what appears to be an engine of some sort.

The only sound that breaks the silence on this mid-December morning comes from the blaze; an uncanny pop and crackle.

He pushes his brown hair out of his face, exposing his dark blue eyes. Richard ponders, in my thirty-nine years of existence, *I have never seen anything; like this.* Pinching his chin as he stares at the site.

In the distance, puffs of dust rise to the sky. A caravan of vehicles heads toward the crash site. "Rogers, I need you to secure the east side perimeter. Make sure that no civilians have access to this accident."

Lieut. Col. Rogers crosses his arms over his chest and glares towards Richard, making sure to gaze past him, rather than at Richard. Leisurely Rogers walks to the east side boundary.

It didn't seem to matter what Richard said; he always came across as though he was barking orders. He had spent many years educating himself to reach the position that he obligates now; countless hours of scholarship. He would have joined the military earlier, but they rejected him for active duty because he needed to wear hearing aids; in both ears. They called the situation a 4-F classification. The funny thing is, he can perceive everything because of his listening device, so his other choice remained the GS program. Yes, he ranks higher than a Lieut. Col. although a GS 14 is still civilian, the resentment he is required to deal with because of his position nevertheless got under his skin.

Richard glimpses off into the distance, his eyebrows raise and he realizes they are heading straight towards the site. He can see it's a camera, crew. *Oh great,* he thinks, *Bonnie Brigantine, from Channel 8 News; does she ever give up?*

Bonnie would not concede. She did not care how long it took to find the killer of her sister. She has escalated her investigations and has become downright annoying. A warpath mentality fills her mind until she became obsessive. Even investigations into the military absorb her thinking. *What are they up too?*

A Sphere containing writings on it slightly glows. The illumination captures Richard's attention. He pulls out a handkerchief from his pocket and picks up the round object. He begins to inspect the *Sphere,* and can comprehend that there is some writing on the outside. It appears to be the size of a golf ball but is much heavier, almost too dense. The engraving seems to be in German, but not any German that Richard, who speaks five languages, recognizes. He ponders, searching his mind but can't place the dialect.

He wants to put the Sphere in his pocket so the item would go undetected from the camera crew, he wraps the cloth around the object. The news team is making real time, to the crash site. Richard hopes that they do not possess binoculars. With sleight-of-hand, the sphere slides into his pocket and Richard turns toward Sgt. Witkowski.

"Sgt. Witkowski, cordon off the area to the west. Make sure to create a barrier to keep out the news crew from the site," Richard points toward the direction.

"Yes, sir," raising his hand, he salutes him while he stiffens his body. He returns his hand to his back.

"Do not under any circumstances reveal what you witness here, to any news media," Richard said.

"No sir, I will not tell them anything," Witkowski said, as he tightens his fists, and his eyebrows begin to furrow. He takes a healthy posture, his chiseled chin, and very short flattop make an intimidating presence.

"No, tell them, that one of our unmanned rockets had a mishap."

"Yes, sir."

Sgt. Witkowski forces the news crew to turn around and leave the area. While Rogers makes his way to the other side and secures the east side of the accident.

"I am a Lieut. Col., I should not be taking orders from a GS 14," Rogers says under his breath. Skinny man that he is, with beady brown eyes, he sports a hostile smile as he twists his mouth in a sour expression.

Richard knew that look all too well; he has seen it countless times.

The fire team hoses down the spaceship until an overflow of the white chemical pools along a gorge next to the craft. Smoke rises above and dissipates into the sky. The crackle of the fire stops. The squeal of brakes halt.

The ambulance crew pulls the vehicle up to the site, steps out and unloads a gurney.

"Sir, you must put on this hazmat uniform, and wear a mask," motions the ambulance driver.

Grabbing the suit Richard begins the task of climbing into the bulky, confining contraption. He places the headgear over his face, "Okay, I've got it."

After the area is secure, military squad open the hatch and remove the bodies inside. The military ambulance loads them into the truck as they attempt to find any signs of life. The crew is wearing hazmat uniforms in case there should be any blood-borne viruses.

The space crew's uniform is foreign looking garb; *maybe German* thinks Richard. *What the hell are the Germans up to?* The clothing and headgear seem much more advanced than anything Richard has seen before.

Richard moves closer, lifting the fabric between his fingers. "I want you to do a full medical with this crew and report back to me as quickly as possible."

"As soon as we figure out what happened, I will personally contact you, sir."

The clean-up crew arrives and hoses Richard down. He removes the protective gear and places it into a pile.

Sgt. Witkowski walks up to Richard. "Sir, we just received a radio message. You have been called to the debriefing room ASAP."

Meanwhile, the ambulance crew has finished loading the bodies and proceed to the top-secret medical facility. Once there, they should be able to discover more information about the team.

A Nellis Air Force Jeep picks up Mr. Clary and drives him back on base to the interrogation area. With all the excitement, Richard completely forgot about the Sphere in his jacket.

Finally arriving at the building, he walks down the long corridor, turning a corner which leads to the debriefing room.

He stands at the door and takes a deep breath as he turns the knob to enter. Upon opening the door, he can detect the complete chaos. Personnel and senior level, scientific and professional, and Defense intelligence are in attendance. (HQE), also known as the Highly Qualified Experts, are walking to and fro with top-secret folders in their hands. File drawers are flinging open and folders tossed about with urgency.

A huge monitor, occupying the majority of the wall, is being studied and viewed. Paying close attention to the red flashing lights; the men begin analyzing any foreign invasions. "General, we don't visualize anything showing up on the monitor," said the military analyst.

Richard takes his seat and thinks, *the table always makes me feel like the Knights of the Roundtable.*

"Mr. Clary. Do you have any information for us?" barks, General Harshman.

"At this point sir, my observation is that the crew of this spaceship are dead. Analyzing the spacecraft and their uniforms I can only surmise that the Germans must bear some involvement."

"The Germans, oh hell not that again," Harshman said. He bangs his fist on the table. Thud!

The head ambulance coordinator steps into the room. He motions to Richard, who stands up and proceeds to meet him at the door. "Have you found out anything about the crew yet?" Richard asked as he glances around the room studying everyone.

"Well sir, they seem to be human; nobody has survived. The technology they have seems far more advanced, than anything I have seen before."

"Really?" Richard made eye contact.

"X-rays show damage to the Medulla Oblongata."

"Thank you. That will be all."

"Well man, do we have any more information to go on?" Harshman asked, his eyebrows creased deeply.

"There seems to be some damage to their brains, sir."

"Okay, Mr. Clary, I know you are going on your vacation, so I'll see you in two weeks. Please inform my secretary where you can be reached."

Richard heads to his office while General Harshman proceeds to grill the rest of the team.

His phone begins to ring, and he can see that it is his daughter. "Hi Crystal, I am heading out now. I should be home in forty-five minutes."

"Hey, Dad, I saw you on the news. Bonnie Brigantine said that 'the military is trying to hide something.'"

"We are not attempting to conceal anything; she possess a big imagination. There is just a small accident over here; nothing to worry about."

"Okay Dad, I got everything ready for our trip. See you soon, bye."

"Goodbye, Crystal."

Crystal is actually excited about the trip. She loves skiing with her dad, and she can use some time away. Her mother; Kathy, passed away one year ago of cancer. Also, her best friend Julia lost her life at the hands of a serial killer. She died shortly after Crystal's mom. Since then, she devises to hold her and her father together.

The bags are packed, and Crystal loads them into the burnt orange van. Crystal takes out her checklist: maps, ice chest, ski boots, skis, bib overalls, three suitcases, and, of course, the Bota bag.

Richard pulls into the driveway. He can perceive that the garage is already open, and Crystal waves at him. He pulls in alongside the van. "Hey Dad, I am going over the checklist."

"If we leave now, we should be able to make it to your grandma's, by 9:00 P.M," Richard said.

"Okay Dad, I am ready to go," she said, grabbing her coat.

Richard steps into the house, checking the windows and doors securing the locks. Now he is ready to go. They hop into the van and head out. They will make it just in time, for the opening of the ski season. Ogden, Utah is about nine hours away. The gateway to Snowbasin, Powder Mountain, and Wolf Mountain ski resorts is right at the mouth of Ogden Canyon. His parent's home is only fifteen minutes from the ski lodge.

Historically, Ogden played a great part in the development of the transcontinental railroad. Just northwest of the city is the Golden Spike National Historic site. This site commemorates the completion of the railroads of Central Pacific and Union Pacific. This marked the end of the American frontier.

Crystal loved the Ogden Canyon, in the springtime her grandparents, Grace, and John would take her out on Sunday drives. They would enterprise through the Canyon as the river would flow under the bridges below and they continued their way farther into the mountain. To the left, she could see the splendid waterfall as water trickled down and hit the rocks. The stones would shine and glisten as light reflected from the sun, and then the stream would make her way to the river. Crystal could almost imagine the men working on the railroads that followed along the journey. The tracks gave her a real sense of history, and she loved antiquity. They would pull up to a particular spot, where her grandparents would pick watercress. They would later make sandwiches with the green leafy plant.

In the summer time, Crystal, her mom, and dad would go water skiing at Pineview Lake. The water was so crystal clear; the bottom of the lake was in plain view. Yes, Ogden Canyon had been a big part of their lives; the happiest ones.

"Crystal, what are you thinking about?"

"Oh Dad, I was just thinking about all the wonderful times we've enjoyed, up in the Ogden Canyon."

"Yeah, we acquired some memorable adventures there."

They were at the halfway mark, so Richard decided to stop for gas. There was quite a bit of snow on the pine trees and bushes. The snowplow has cleared the roads, and the weather report is decent. Although there would be plenty of snow for the ski lift; it has stopped pelting down.

Crystal, brushes her long blond hair, away from her shoulder. Placing her purse there, she heads for the store. Following right behind her father, they enter the restrooms. Now is the time to pick up a few snacks and another cup of coffee. "Twenty dollars on pump three please," Richard said.

Returning to the van, Richard proceeds to fill up the tank while Crystal gets in. The sun is beginning to go down, and she can witness the shadows created by the mountains. The snow has dusted all the trees. Feeling the chill of the cold; Crystal could not wait to get to her grandmother.

Her grandparents, always keep the house warm and toasty. Crystal could already imagine the fire blazing in the family room. The thought brought comfort to her.

"So what exactly happened at the base today?" she said, rubbing her hands together to keep them warm.

"Like I told you, it was just a small accident," he said, twitching back and forth in his seat.

"Did anybody get hurt?"

"None of our men got injured."

Richard wanted to tell her the whole shebang, but he was not authorized to do so. Sometimes he just wished that he could tell everybody what he did. If they only knew that the military already hold the capability to use handheld devices to speak to each other and view them on the screen, they would be shocked. Alternatively, that they monitored anyone at any given time, with a device like this; they would be furious. He is a systems analyst, computer programmer, and he can speak and read five different languages. He specialized in various dialects so as to be able to decipher messages and codes. That way they could be one step ahead of the other countries. As of late he has actually been researching and studying the capability for *time travel.*

He recently received a master's degree in physics and mathematics. Also, now with what he had observed today, he thinks that the bodies they discovered from the crash may actually be from another time; possibly from the future. Richard isn't sure, but he suspects that is the case.

"Dad, we are getting closer; Lagoon is up ahead," Crystal said. Lagoon Amusement Park closed for the winter is plastered across the main entrance. She reflected on the paddleboats on the lake inside the park.

"Crystal, pop in the music tape," Richard said. *I want to hold your hand,* could be heard in the background. They start singing the song.

Lastly, they arrive in Ogden. They pull up to the house and glimpse that the lights are on. Richard and Crystal grab their suitcases and proceed inside.

Grace and John greet them with a warm embrace and kisses.

Crystal studies the two-story brick home with a basement. The house built in 1904 was the first firehouse in Ogden. The molding around the doorways and walls gave it that incredibly antique-looking style. The basement shelves stocked with Grandma's canned cherries and Grandpa's fruit leather. They had lived through the Great Depression, so they always have well-stocked shelves. They never waste anything and utilized cherries and plums from their trees.

Richard takes their suitcases upstairs to the second floor. There are two bedrooms. One of them is quite small and overlooks the backyard. The other room is large and overlooks the front yard. Resting the luggage on the bed, Richard can spy out the front window, down to the street and starts thinking about the first time he met Kathy. *I was rolling a tire down the street, to get the gaping hole repaired at the auto shop when I noticed her standing out in her front yard, smiling and looking so enchanting. She had medium brown hair, alluring blue eyes with flax that sparkled, and a tiny, attractive frame. I struck up a conversation with her and asked her out. After that moment, we spent as much time as we could, together. That moment seems so long ago, and now she is gone.* Tears welled up in his eyes. He thought; *I have to stop agonizing over this.*

Looking away from the window, rubbing the small pools of water that slid down his cheek, he turns and walks toward the stairs. He made his way down to the den.

His parents built a warm fire in the family room. Watching their favorite Lawrence Welk Show; as usual, they gathered around the TV together and caught up on the most recent news about their friends and family.

"Well, we better get some shut eye, so we can get up early tomorrow and hit the ski slopes," Richard said. He rubbed his eyes.

"Okay, we will see you in the morning," Grandma said.

"I love you, Grandma."

"Love you too sweetie."

"Good night, Dad."

"Good night, my son."

In the morning, Richard and Crystal get up early. Grace is already making breakfast for them. She always puts out quite a spread; making sure that everyone has a good meal before he or she start their day. John reads the newspaper as he eats his breakfast. "Richard, it says here that there was an accident near Nellis Air Force Base. Is that right?"

"Yeah, it was nothing Dad, an unmanned spacecraft. No one got hurt." Thinking to himself, *I am lying through my teeth.* He hated to lie, especially to his dad. However, that was his job, and he could not break protocol.

"What time will you be back?" Grace asked.

"We should be home by 5:00 P.M. at the latest," Richard replied.

Richard and Crystal check all of their gear and make sure that nothing is missing. "Okay, we're ready. See you guys when we get back," Crystal said.

They wave goodbye and make their way up the Canyon. In a clearing off to the right Crystal spots a female deer. She is graceful and identifies the vehicle instantly. The Doe lopes off into the forest and out of sight.

"Did you notice a deer, Dad?"

"I did; she is beautiful."

Richard pops in a music tape, as they make their way up the mountain. Clumps of snow covered the beautiful Pine and Aspen trees. As the weight of the snow exceeded, he can see it fall from the trees, floating in the wind.

"Crystal, I need you to go to the back of the van and help create some traction by jumping back and forth."

"Okay Dad, how is this?" She jumps back and forth, the object, Richard has in his coat pocket rolls out towards Crystal, and it pops openly. Suddenly the sphere creates a bright light engulfing Richard and Crystal. In the background they can hear the music, *love loves me do.*

They instantly transfigure to 1964, in London, England inside a bar. A very young band happens to be playing that night. Richard having been in a seated position, begins to fall. Crystal, beholding the sphere rolling towards her tries to grab the object in her hands, as she notices her father start to fall. She struggles to get to him before he lands. She reaches him just in time to break his fall. They are both now sitting on the floor.

Crystal stares into her father's eyes and asks, "What just happened, Dad?"

Stunned by the sudden loss of the seat and his daughter breaking his fall, he stares into her dark blue eyes. Upon doing so, he can observe the main stage behind her and on that stage is the band, *who* at this point are staring back at them. Had the Sphere created a bright light and grabbed their attention?

"I am not sure, but keep a low profile," Richard said.

Looking around, they stand up. "Dad I can spot a free table why don't we just sit down?" Glancing around uneasily they walk towards the table.

"That is a magnificent idea, let's just try to blend in," he said.

"Dad, I noticed this round thing coming at me and pop open and then there was this intense, penetrating light, and that light engulfed us." As her fingers touched her parted lips.

He concealed his face as he put his elbow on the table and leaned down covering one eye. "Where is it now?"

"I slipped it right here in my pocket." She pointed to her coat.

"Okay Crystal, just leave it there, don't take it out, don't touch it!"

"It must be some time travel object. It must possess some sound wave mechanism that can transfigure us to a different point in history," Richard explained. "This is fantastic!"

"Wow, I see the group live, and I think we are in London, England," Crystal said.

The band decides to take a break. George steps off the stage. He makes his way towards the couple. "What was that fairy light; it blinded me?"

"Oh, that was just my flashlight; I dropped it," Richard said. Hoping that would settle his curiosity.

"Flashlight?" He looked confused and said, "Oh you mean torch, I get it."

"Are you Americans?" he asked. Their attire seems foreign to him.

"Yes, we are visiting some relatives."

"Well, your bevy is on me."

"Thank you."

"The band will be leaving for America tomorrow." He handed her some tickets for the tube.

"Thank you so much," Crystal said.

Richard has a star-struck look on his face. He shook his hand and thanked him for a drink. He begins to quiz him about his life and where they plan on going. Meanwhile, Crystal sips her beverage and listens intently. The evening is winding down, and the band begins to pack up their instruments.

"What should we do next, Dad?" With her eyes bright and confused.

"We probably should head to Kent, England."

"Why Kent?"

"Your great-grandparents still live there; they might be able to assist us."

"You mean Great Grandma and Grandpa Tag?"

"Yes, your great grandfather Bert is in the Royal Army."

"Hi, my name is Tom, I could not help but overhear that you know the Tags." He searches their faces, he felt like he has encountered Crystal before.

"Yes, they are relatives of ours," Richard said.

"Well, my mums gaff is right next door to them, and I happen to be going there right after work. I plan to spend the weekend with my mum," Tom said. "Would you like a ride?"

"Thank you, we will take you up on that offer," Richard replied.

Walking out to the car, Tom studies the curve of Crystal's mouth. The faint aroma of flowers drifts to him and he inhales the fragrance. The scent brought a memory to mind. *I remember her from the college class in Virginia. But how can that be I am the only time traveler; ever. Or am I?* He motioned to open the door, but Crystal had already reached up for the handle. Her hand touches his, which sent an electric charge through their bodies. A burning desire awakened him.

"Sorry, I could get that for you," he said. Recoiling quickly to avoid any contact.

"I am fine, I can open my own door," she snapped. Feeling the heat that overcame her in space they shared. *What was that?*

Opening the door, she got in the back of the red and tan Rolls-Royce Phantom.

Richard climbs into the front. "Is this a 1960 Phantom?" He lays his hand on the seat to caress the leather.

Tapping the console. "You know your cars," replied Tom.

They made their way through London. They finally start to drive through the countryside. It is dark outside, but the moon illuminates the forest so they can see some of the trees with laden moss hanging down. Off to the left, they catch a glimmer of Leeds Castle.

She could just imagine the king and his men galloping through the countryside on their horses; carrying their family crest flag.

"Look, Dad, Leeds Castle. Mom used to come out to the big green area and play as a child."

"Yes, we are about two blocks away now," he replied.

"How long will you be on holiday with the Tag family?"

"We will not be able to stay very long, but at least for a few days," Richard replied.

He looked to be about twenty-one years old. He is well-dressed and very English. Crystal could not help but admire his deep blue eyes he parades, they seem to flash and sparkle as he gazes at Crystal. Of which he does a lot through the rearview mirror. His medium light brown hair has a slight wave to the strands. She found him extremely attractive, and she loves his accent. *How can I feel this way about a complete stranger?*

Tom knew it was her, viewing her from the mirror, with her long blond hair which smells like Jasmine flowers and the blue eyes with white flax that seem to light up when she glanced at him.

"Well, here we are if you need anything I'll be next door," Tom said.

"Thank you for the ride. We really do appreciate it," Richard said.

Tom steps into his mother's home; meanwhile Richard and Crystal walk next door. "Okay Crystal, let me do the talking."

"No problem Dad, I do not know what I would say anyway." She sported a bewildered look.

Richard rapped on the door. The lights came on, and Great Grandma Tag answered the door. "Richard what are you doing here?" Elizabeth asked. "Is that Kathy?"

"Hi, I know this timely hour is late, but I was hoping we could stay the night?" Richard asked.

"Of course come on in," she replied.

They sat down on the couch in the living room. Bert enters the room. "Richard what are you doing here?"

"I do not know how to say this," Richard said.

"You look older," Bert said.

"Bert, this will be difficult to imagine, but I am thirty-nine years old, and this is not Kathy, it is our daughter Crystal."

"What in heaven's name?" Bert replied. He looked them up and down.

"Somehow we have traveled through time, I know this sounds crazy but look closely at us."

Elizabeth came closer. She examines Crystal and then looked at Richard. "Dear God, you are older."

"What on earth happened, Richard?" Bert asked.

Crystal pulled the object out of her pocket and gave it to her dad.

"I acquired this *Sphere* in the Nevada desert not far from Nellis Air Force Base after a spaceship crashed in the wilderness. It was 1983 and it somehow transported us here."

"My dear, you look so much like your mum," Elizabeth said. "I thought that you lightened your hair or something."

"I remembered that you studied German hieroglyphics and would like your opinion," Richard said.

Bert examines the sphere without touching it. "It is German alright."

"It must have some way of fixing on a date," Richard said.

"Or it could be sound waves, what sound did you hear before it transported you?" Bert asked.

"My favorite band and then they were right in front of me," Richard said.

"Yeah, it can get a fix on latitude and longitude by sound, but it must be open. It must have some kind of the sound device to pick up the sound waves," Bert said.

"I don't want to experiment with it tonight. There are too many variables so we will try tomorrow after we get some rest," Richard said.

"You can stay in the guest room upstairs. There is a sitting room adjacent to the bedroom, and it has a couch that pulls out into a bed," Elizabeth said.

Richard thinks; *it is best to stay together in case our time travel is a fluke, at least we will be together.* "I think we should stay close, just in case," Richard said.

Crystal appropriated the bed and Richard unfolds the couch. They could make out Leeds Castle from the bedroom window. "I think we will be okay, just stick close together in case there is an element that we don't know about."

"Okay Dad," Crystal said. She continues to gaze out the window. An arch between her eyes shows the growing concern on her face.

Richard hugged her. "Don't worry honey, I won't let anything happen to you." He mulls over the events of the day, keeping in mind that he has a time travel object. An epiphany occurs to him Kathy would be seventeen years old right now. He has a hard time sleeping because he keeps wondering if he is alive right now in 1964 in Kent, England would he also be alive and nineteen years of age in Ogden, Utah?

The possibilities were endless and he would have to research and take notes so he can keep up with the probabilities. One thing is for sure he now has hope; something that he has been short of the past few years.

Chapter 2

MERRY OLD ENGLAND

EARLY IN THE MORNING Crystal and Richard are awake. "Well, it looks like we are still in Kent, England," said Richard. "At least we did not jump through time; in our sleep." Pulling the blanket back, he sits up, stretching his arms above his head. "Ah." He steps out of bed and walks to the sunlight.

He glances out the window and thinks about how his beloved Kathy had once lived there, and she probably slept in that very bed. She was only four years of age when she came to America. He would have never met her if she had not. *Was it all the bombing during World War II that caused her to get cancer later on in life?*

Much of the house is built of stone and brick. The craftsmanship explained how it survived the bombing during the war. Although the foundation has a slight crack on the back end of the home, the rest of the abode is untouched and unblemished. The wood flooring shines as the light from the window touches the floor base. Birds come to rest on the window overhang, peeking in looking for crumbs. He found it difficult to believe this was once a war-torn area. Now peaceful and almost poetic, with birds chirping, light shining as though no evil thing could creep in and yet at one-time doodlebugs flew over threatening to destroy such beauty. V-1 flying bomb knew all too well by the British inhabitants as *the doodlebugs*, but allies called it the buzz bomb. Many recall the burning bodies falling from buildings where unsuspecting victims met their death because of those bombs.

Elizabeth raps on the door. "I've made you some breakfast."

"Thank you, we will be down in just a few minutes," said Crystal. Wrapping a robe around her.

They make their way down to the kitchen. Elizabeth is busy preparing breakfast; she has just finished making some fresh apricot-caramel scones. Pulling them out of the oven, sliding them onto a plate, she pours them each a cup of tea and puts some cream on the table. Sitting down a plate for each of them, she puts a smidgen of Devonshire cream on both of them. Returning to the counter she picks up the plate of scones and moves them to the table. "You must be hungry after your adventure, I hope this will help."

"Good morning, I think I found something that might be of some interest to you, Richard. While working for the Royal Army, I found an ancient book; I tucked it away. However, now it might be able to answer some questions," said Bert.

Richard studies the writing and realizes there is a drawing of the *Sphere* in the book. He is amazed that it is something timeworn instead of something futuristic. "Where did you find this Bert?"

"Believe it or not, I found it buried not far from Stonehenge." Holding his chin high as he stands over Richard with his legs spread wide sporting a knowing grin. "I was particularly aghast when I saw the *Sphere,* and I recalled the drawing in this book."

"The more I study the language on here it seems that it is Gaelic. Sure it is a little different but not much. They did not want anyone to learn the dialect and did everything he or she could; keep it from being taught in the schools, and that actually made people leave Ireland and England," said Richard.

"Yes, it starts to make some sense now," said Bert. "Gaelic and German share some ancient roots in the word."

Crystal is hungrier than she thought, and the scones that her great grandma made are delicious. She devours the scones and thoroughly enjoys the Devonshire cream. "You mean to tell me that, they were trying to keep this a secret?" Crystal said. Turning her head to the side and looking down at the floor. "That means that someone else knows about this besides us." She looked back up at them.

"We've stumbled on something bigger than you could imagine, and if this got into the wrong hands it could mean complete chaos for our world," said Richard.

"Whatever you do Richard, make sure that this Sphere does not leave your hands. Otherwise, it could be a disaster," said Bert. "And keep this cover on the book so that no one can see what it is." He picks up the book and wraps the cover over it.

"Dear, I have some pictures of your mum that I want you to have." Elizabeth carries a photo album over to the table. She lightly set it down in front of her. "This is a picture of your mum's christening, which took place at Canterbury Cathedral."

Tears form in her eyes. "Thank you."

"This other picture was taken at the Dover Cliffs." She slides the image out of the album.

"You can see the English Channel in that picture," Bert said as he pointed to the photo.

"Mother told me you swam the English Channel, is that right?"

"Yes," said Bert.

"Was it hard?"

"Bloody cold it was."

Crystal helps clean up the kitchen, washing the dishes and putting the food away. She heads upstairs to get cleaned up and dressed.

When she is finished, Richard does the same.

Elizabeth shows Crystal her flower garden and shares stories about her grandmother, the war, and much of the history of England. Crystal hangs on her every word, not wanting to miss any details.

"My daughters Molly and Heather became so desensitized by the war they thought they would die any moment, so their plan was to go to the Armory Hall to dance the night away with their boyfriends.

One night the Germans sent over the doodlebugs and one fell through the ceiling of the room and to their surprise did not go off. Perplexed, they—then began to dance again as though nothing had happened." Handing her some flowers. "After the war when your Nana Molly got married and your mum was born, they decided to leave for America."

Walking back into the house they place the tulips in a vase. Red, pink and white flowers liven up the kitchen.

Bert and Elizabeth have to leave for work. They inform Richard and Crystal that they can stay as long as they need to. "We will be back about 5:00 P.M.; we will understand if you are not here. I will keep a journal, and save it for our ancestral records just in case," said Bert.

"We probably will not be here when you get back. Thanks so much for all the help, and if everything goes well we will laugh about this in the future," said Richard.

Crystal hugged her great grandma and grandpa. "I am glad that I got to meet you when I am older, and I can appreciate it."

Elizabeth and Bert hugged them both and wished them well. They get into their car, and they wave goodbye. "Lovey, I hope this works out for them," said Elizabeth.

"Me too," said Bert.

"I've been thinking about this a lot Crystal, if I can get this time travel object working properly for us, I have this idea." Richard's mouth began to curve up.

"What is it, Dad?" Staring intently into his eyes.

"I've devoted my life to the government job possibly spent too much time investing in that instead of my family and I lost your mom along the way. If it is at all possible to go forward in time and see if they have found a cure for cancer—"

"Oh Dad, could it even be possible that we could take it back with us? And then give it to Mom before she died?" Holding her breath and raising her eyebrows. Offering a questionable gaze; smiling.

"Remember what I said sweetie, anything is possible." As he gazed back at her with a glimmer of hope.

"Yeah, I remember you said, 'if it is impossible let's do it because nothing is impossible; if you set your mind to it.' " Determined more than ever to make this a reality, she tucks the photos of her mom in her pocket.

"Yesterday we were just going snow skiing in Ogden, Utah. Now we are in England and it is 1964," replied Richard.

"I miss Mom so much, and I feel like I got a double whammy," Crystal said. "And since 'nothing is impossible' Dad, can we save Julia too?" Gazing up at him with her big blue eyes.

"That might be a little more dangerous," said Richard. As his voice deepened.

"I know Dad, but if we can do this, then let's just do it." Walking up to him she put her arms around his waist and holds him tight.

"Okay Crystal, that one might be tricky but anything is possible, so let's do it." He put his arms around her shoulders and patted her back.

"We need to figure out what to take for this trip, I do not know exactly how to pack for this." Crystal looks around and realizes that, they do not have anything that they brought with them. She checks the photos of her mom into her pocket.

"Bert has already figured that out for us. That is what those two duffel bags are for."

Crystal rummages through the duffel bags. She finds foreign coins, rope, a few different IDs and several different types of clothing so as to allow them to blend in. There is also a canteen full of water and beef jerky.

"We will experiment with this Sphere inside, but I need you to be as close to me as possible," said Richard. "Do you understand me?"

"Don't worry Dad I do not want to be left behind; anywhere."

"Okay, if I apply pressure on this pinhole we should be able to override the sound waves."

"I have a bobby pin. Would that work?" Crystal replied.

"Yes, that will work just fine."

"Now if I do not have enough time to adjust for the latitude and longitude, we might make a quick stop somewhere that we did not plan on. So just follow my lead and stick close."

"I am ready Dad."

Richard applies pressure to the pinhole that allows the *Sphere* to open. Now he can see the latitude and longitude marks inside the Sphere. He tries to adjust but unfortunately he pulls them a little farther back in time instead of forward. Suddenly just like before, the flashes of light surround them and they are pulled back in time. Now standing in the same spot that they were except now the house is not standing any longer, and they are in a beautiful green meadow.

"Wow Dad, look how beautiful it is." Crystal is circumspect, she waits and smiles, "I can still see Leeds Castle."

Underneath a tree about five paces from them, a man is sitting and writing on a scroll. He looks up and sees them. The man walks closer towards them. Richard upon seeing this turns to Crystal and says, "Just continue walking in the opposite direction."

"Who goes there?" The man yells out.

"Richard Tag, Sir."

"Richard Tag from Tag Island?"

"Yes, Sir."

"Well man, what are you doing out here?"

"Sir, we were mugged and lost our way, but we know where we are going now; sorry to intrude."

"Don't you recognize me?" Henry said.

Richard returns and begins to bend, "Your Majesty." As he motions for Crystal to bow also.

"Good God man you are my second cousin, get up. We need to get you inside; both of you need a change of clothing and a bath."

"I am so glad you recognize us."

"This must be Isabella, your daughter?" He looked her up and down.

"Yes, this is Isabella Tag." She bowed a curtsy.

"Isabella, this is King Henry VIII. He is our third cousin."

"You look a fright in those trousers, did they steal your gown miss?"

"Yes, Sir, all of my clothing Sir."

King Henry motions to his man-servant. "Get my cousin cleaned up and find a maid-servant for Isabella."

"Yes, Your, Majesty."

Chapter 3

INSIDE THE CASTLE

GWENDOLYN HER MAIDSERVANT LEADS Crystal to the guest living quarters. She follows up the stone staircase to the second floor. Elaborate paintings of King Henry VIII and his beautiful Queen Catherine of Aragon line the walls. She realizes that this is the Tudor dynasty. Although the castle is, very elegant Crystal knows that they are in great danger.

King Henry VIII is famous for divorcing his first wife, Queen Catherine. And is best recognized for his role in the separation of the Church of England from the Roman Catholic Church to receive that annulment. It became the desolation of the monastery and his establishment as the supreme head of the Church of England.

He would go on to have six marriages. One of his wives was not so lucky. Anne Bolin, his second wife, was beheaded. His third wife Jane Seymour died after giving birth to their first son.

Although Crystal is excited to be inside the castle and to experience what it is like back then, she is also in fear they would be found out.

Once the king realizes that Crystal is not Isabella, he most assuredly will have them put to death.

The bath water rises to the top, and a mixture of lavender and gardenias occupy in the air. Her nostrils breathe in the lovely aroma as she soaks in the Golden tub. Gwendolyn washes her hair in the most beautifully scented Aragon oil from the Indies. And then she lays out a very extravagant green silk gown. Her maidservant begins the task of decorating her hair in the most exquisite updo with beautiful soft curls.

Crystal sits in front of the mirror, as Gwendolyn fusses with her hair. "Is Father nearby?"

"I believe he is in the east wing." She places the last hairpin on Crystal's hair and adds two diamond hair combs.

"Gwendolyn, you are talented."

"Thank you." She motions for Crystal to stand up, so she can lower the gown over her. Then she completes her makeup.

Crystal looks in the mirror; she turns to the left and then to the right. "What a beautiful gown."

"And now for the finishing touch." Gwendolyn fastens the emerald necklace around her neck.

Gwendolyn has light brown hair and blue eyes, which matches her blue silk gown. She smiles at Crystal as though she is pleased with her workmanship. "Now you are a fully presentable young lass."

While Gwendolyn leaves the room to pick up more towels, Crystal puts the picture of her mother and the other items into her bra.

Meanwhile on the other side of the castle Richard's manservant has just finished with him. Richard feels quite silly in his outfit but does not make a fuss. He feels like he is dressing for a play. The greatest performance of his life and is hoping to pull it off. His clothing is bulky which makes it easy to conceal the book and the *Sphere*.

They are both led down to the dining room by the servants. The King is already present with his Queen and a few of his friends. Crystal and Richard sit next to each other. He whispers, "As soon as we have an opportunity we need to find a quiet part of the castle."

"I think the church might be silent, it is down the hall," says Crystal. "I saw it on my way down here." She motions with her hand pointing in the direction of the church.

"That is a perfect idea. When we are finished eating, we can excuse ourselves to go pray."

The minstrels are playing music in the background, and the King begins to sing, "Past time with good company I love and shall unto I die."

"How beautiful," Crystal said. Admiring his voice which displayed a sound ear for harmony.

"Oh, you like that? I wrote that," said Henry. Puffing out his chest in a proud gesture.

"You wrote that?" Crystal said. "I love it." She is amazed that the king is so talented, and the song seems like such a sensitive song. Of all the history that she has read about King Henry VIII she never once realized that he also is a songwriter and poet.

The servants enter the room with a bountiful feast. Everyone is drinking and eating and making merriment. Sir George of Canterbury keeps winking at Crystal, which makes her very uncomfortable. He asks her to dance, and she obliged. She did not want to cause any suspicion, so she went along.

His hands seemed to roam along the small of her back. She winced at the touch of it, but he did not notice. He was used to getting everything he wanted but was well aware not to upset the King.

"My dear King, it is time for our evening prayer, we shall return momentarily," Richard announced. Looking intently at Crystal on the dance floor. He spotted her flawless movements and he made his way across the floor.

"May I have a moment with my daughter, Sir George?"

"Most certainly."

Finally, Richard has a private minute with Crystal, and they scurry down the hall to the church. They hope that their departure was not observed, which would allow them more time. "Close the door," said Richard.

"Dad you look so silly in that outfit, Ha, Ha, Ha."

"We have to keep moving; I know I look ridiculous, hold my hand." At that moment he pushes the bobby pin into the pinhole, the *Sphere* opens, and he turns it in the opposite direction. Just like before the light engulfs them, and as they transfigure the king opens up the church doors and sees the bright lights overwhelm them and take them away.

"What in heaven's name just happened?" said the King. Being completely baffled by what he just saw. "I must have had too much to drink." He continues to stare at the light and then back to his goblet clutched in his trembling hand.

Richard and Crystal have safely made it out of the castle and have landed in the year 2035. In New York in front of the Presbyterian Hospital where Dr. Slavic has mastered his antidote for cancer. Billboards surrounding the whole city have Dr. Slavic's picture up on the poster with the slogan, "Cure for Cancer."

"Dad, how did you know that Dr. Slavic would have a cure in the future?" She stared him straight in the eye.

"I've been following his research and he seems to be the only one that has a grasp of what it would take to cure this disease." Pushing his hair away from his forehead.

"That was a close call, the king entered the church just as we transfigured. He would have surely killed us," she said. Her hair disarray as it carelessly fell to her shoulders.

"By the look on his face, he is probably wondering if he had some religious experience, ha, ha, ha," he chuckled.

"Ha, ha, ha, yeah did you see the look on his face, it was priceless." She regained control of her hair and pinned it back with the diamond combs.

"We must gain entry into the medical supply room; they may have some lab coats in there," said Richard. Viewing the employees through the window.

"I do not even think that a lab coat could cover up this!" Crystal replied. As she looked down at her gown and realizes that, she has taken off with the crown jewels too. The gems sparkled.

"That gives me an idea. New York is famous for the finest jewelers, we might be able to sell those emeralds."

"Yeah, that would give us some money, we could get a room and something to wear."

"Or we could take those diamond combs in your hair, and sell them and just pick up some clothes and sneak in," suggested Richard. "I think you better take off that emerald necklace and put it away."

Richard and Crystal make their way to the nearest jewelry store. The shop is still open, and they ring the buzzer. A small man with Jewish dreads hanging down the sides of his face allows them to enter. "How may I help you?"

"I was hoping that you might be interested in purchasing these diamond combs they are a family heirloom from the 1500s. King Henry VIII once owned them," said Richard.

The jeweler examines the combs and knows that he has a rare find. "I can give you ten thousand dollars for the combs, that is as high as I can go," replies the jeweler.

"That will be okay."

Counting the money he hands the cash to him. "There you go. It has been a pleasure doing business with you. If you have any other family heirlooms to sell, please contact us at this number."

"Thank you."

Richard and Crystal leave the jewelry store. "Dad I cannot believe that we got that much money for those combs."

"They are a collector's item, probably worth even more than that," said Richard. "Now we need to get out of these clothes and find ourselves some hospital scrubs and a lab coat."

"Look, Dad, there's a uniform store down at the end of the street." Crystal raises her hand and points to the shop.

Walking down the streets of New York at night when it is starting to get dark can be a little creepy. They reach the uniform store and start shopping around for the perfect getup. They find two lab coats and some scrubs. The clerk is so impressed with their costumes; he makes an even trade. They head back to the hospital as they devise their plan. Watching carefully how the medical staff runs each area.

"Okay Crystal, just walk with me and let me do all the talking, or should I call you Isabella?"

Crystal giggles as she walks next to him. "I kind of like that name." With the new name, she also had a lofty swagger in her step.

Richard checks the information center and discovers that Dr. Slavic is on the third floor. They got on the elevator and made their way to the third floor. As they exit the elevator, Richard heads for one of the patient's room. He picks up the case chart and examines it. Crystal stands quietly next to him. The nurse enters the room. "Hi, you must be Dr. Jordan from Colorado. You were not expected until tomorrow morning," says Nurse Jackie.

"I have an intern who will be assisting me, and I wanted to show her around; to make sure she knew the patient's."

"Mr. Johnson is getting his cancer shot tomorrow, but if you'd like to get an early start I am sure he would not mind; would you Mr. Johnson?"

"The sooner, the better," he replied.

"I will be back with the antidote, just give me five minutes," said Jackie.

The nurse leaves the room and heads for the medicine department. She enters her key code and receives one antidote for cancer. Five minutes later she returns. "Here you go Dr. Jordan, I will be back later to check on Mr. Johnson."

"Thank you, Nurse Jackie." He tries not to make eye contact, by avoiding her gaze.

"Will it hurt Doc?" he asked. Tossing and turning to get comfortable.

"You will not feel a thing," Richard said. As he pretends to give him a shot by giving him a slight pinch on his arm. "You should be feeling better by tomorrow, if not we may have to give you another shot. Now get some rest."

Richard and Crystal leave his room and head straight for the elevator. Their hearts are racing as they go down each floor. Finally, they reach the bottom level and make a beeline for the door. Once outside, they continue walking down the street until they reach the Cashmere

Hotel. Richard checks them into a room. They continue to walk in silence until they are safely tucked away in their hotel room.

"I have never been so afraid in my whole life," said Crystal. Still trembling from the experience. Her hands could not stop shaking.

"Impersonating a doctor, wow I can really get into trouble for that, but your mother is worth it." He has a goal in mind and that kept him going.

"Do you believe that the nurse, she just handed us the antidote, that is crazy wonderful!" Crystal said. Embracing her father as tears of happiness slid down her face.

"Yeah, I am glad she gave it to me since I was shaking with excitement," he replied. Continuing to hug Crystal and wipe her tears away.

"Don't worry, we are almost there."

"I hope the man gets his shot," said Crystal. "He seemed to be in so much pain."

"Don't worry Crystal, I left a note on his chart that he had not received the shot yet."

"I am glad you did that, but they will be looking for us real soon," she replied. Glancing around the room.

"I know, we need to get out of here right now; ready?" he asked.

"I cannot wait to see Mom again, let's go."

"Okay let's make sure that we have everything," he said. "Alright, Crystal hold my hand, here we go."

Richard applies pressure into the pinhole; the *Sphere* opens, and he positions the latitude and longitude and turns the knob back slightly. Just like before they are engulfed by the light and transfigure. However, this time Richard was slightly off and instead of being at his home, they are down the street from his house. It was nighttime, and they went unnoticed. Once they gather their bearings, they head for the residence. They can hardly wait and start to move even faster. Finally, they are at the front door. They open the ingress and run upstairs.

"Is that you Richard?" Kathy said. She laid in a bed full of pain. The room has grown dark.

"Yes, honey it is me." He turns on the light, and he can behold her reclining in bed, looking frail. She is in great agony. He walks up next to her and kisses her softly on her cheek and takes her hand into his. "I do not have much time to explain, but I have an antidote for your cancer." He rolls up her sleeve and begins applying the shot.

"Where did you get it?" Her arm initiates to tingle as warmth fills her veins. Feeling overwhelmed by the sensation.

Crystal stands in the doorway, tears streaming down her face and the biggest smile. "It is a long story Mom, let's just say we're overjoyed to see you." She climbs into bed next to her mom and holds her as she will never let go.

Within a few hours, Kathy is sitting up, the color returning to her cheeks. She smiles and the dullness in her eyes has vanished, it is replaced with a blue sparkle Richard so loved. They spend the next few hours explaining to Kathy, the adventures they encountered over the last few days.

Kathy feels much better, and she has so much energy she decides to get up and make some dinner for her family. She has her appetite back. Laughter fills the kitchen as they each help make the meal for the evening.

"Mom, I want you to just to sit down at the dining table and enjoy this moment while Dad and I finish making you dinner."

Crystal pours her mother a large glass of apple juice and puts it on the table next to her. Meanwhile, Richard finished cooking the chicken fried rice. Now they are all sitting at the table enjoying their meal. Laughing and smiling and savoring their time together. A moment that neither one of them thought they would ever have again.

The doorbell rings...

Chapter 4

NO REST FOR THE WICKED

THE DOORBELL RINGS. "I will get it," said Crystal.

"Wait Crystal, you better let me get that," said Richard. He walks up to the door and he peeked through the peephole and realized who it is. He opened up the ingress and said, "Julia, hurry come on in." He very quickly locked the door behind her.

Crystal saw Julia's face. She rushed to her and wrapped her arms tightly around her, "I've missed you so much Julia."

"What are you talking about? I just saw you yesterday?" A hard visible swallow showed her reluctance.

Richard runs upstairs taking two steps at a time and grabbed his gun, gripping his finger around the handle, knuckles protruding and rushes back downstairs. Then he proceeds to check all of the doors and windows and closes all of the drapes. He checks his pocket to make sure that he still has the *Sphere* in it.

Julia is just shocked, she cannot figure out what is going on. "What is it Richard, why do you have your gun and why are you closing all of the curtains?"

"Crystal. Call nine-one-one," said Richard. He paces back and forth.

"Okay, Dad." She grabbed the phone and frantically dialed.

"Will somebody tell me what's going on?" Kathy said, fixing her gaze on the gun.

"Nine-one-one operators, what is your emergency?"

"There is a man named Rex Munday, who has been stalking and killing women for the past ten years. He has been following a friend, Julia, and we spot him outside of our house right now. We need the police, send an officer and backup, he is very dangerous."

"Are you sure that it is him?" replied the dispatch.

"Oh yes, I saw him with my own eyes; it is him all right," said Crystal. "There was a news clip about him a month ago on channel 8 news."

"The police are on their way, do not hesitate to protect yourself," said the dispatch. "And stay on the line until they arrive, okay?"

"We will not, hesitate that is," replied Crystal. She thought *I would like to bash his head.*

Richard takes Julia and Kathy aside to the living room, "Julia I know this might be hard to believe, but Crystal and I have been able to travel in time. Although it may sound crazy, it is true. Also, the guy who followed you about a week ago is a serial killer named Rex Munday. He is a murderer killing women for at least ten years."

"The one that was following us in the car and was staring at us?" Julia asked.

"Yes," replied Richard.

"Oh my God, now it makes sense the way he stared at us, it was frightening, not normal." She trembled at the thought.

"I know it is hard to believe about the time travel, but look at me, they went forward in time and was able to get an antidote for my cancer. In the past two years I have never looked this good," said Kathy.

"If you can go forward in time, and then back in time, then you know what he is going to do," said Julia.

"Yes, and that is why we must stop him," said Richard.

"The police have informed me they are at your door now," said the operator.

Suddenly there is a knock at the entrance. The officer said, "Mr. Clary, this is the police department. We have secured the area." They are armed and their guns are drawn.

Richard looks through the peephole and he can see the police and their uniforms. He opens up the door and the officer's step inside. "Sir you can put down your gun now."

Richard slowly drops his weapon to the floor and exhales.

Crystal hangs up the phone and walks up to the police officers. She begins to tell them how the man named Rex Munday has been stalking them for months now. She proceeds to give them a description of him and all of the locations that she has seen him.

"Well, he matches the description of the man we have been looking for, we will patrol the area."

"Thank you, officers," said Richard.

The police exit the house and begin a structured patrol.

Richard decides to take some precautions. He loads up the van with blankets and pillows, extra gallons of water and packaged foods that will keep for a while. He makes sure that his gun is close to him at all times. He checked his supply of bullets; repeatedly.

"What are you doing Dad?"

"We do not know when he will strike, but we have one thing on our side; we are prepared. If we have to, we can leave and go to a safe area."

"Where would we go?" said Julia.

"I have not figured that out yet but just give me a little time," Richard said.

Richard pulls out his map and starts studying escape routes and locations that he felt they would be safe at. Also, he measures the latitude and longitude of the areas, just in case he needs to use the *Sphere*.

Meanwhile, Crystal motions Julia to follow her up to her bedroom. "We need to change our clothes."

"You are probably right I cannot run around in a pair of cutoffs and beachcombers, I'll never get away from that guy like this," said Julia.

"Here you can wear my Chemin De Fer button up sailor pants, the blue ones, and those blue sneakers." She laid them out on the bed.

"Okay, but do you have another pair sneakers you can wear?"

"Yeah, don't worry I have those white sneakers and a white button up chemin defer jeans."

"So, how bad is this guy?"

"Look, I do not want to freak you out but this guy is so bad, he has killed at least thirty women."

"From the way that you treated me when I got here, I have this sneaking suspicion that I was one of them." She looks at Crystal with her big blue eyes and her short blond hair and a very frightened look on her face. Her lips and chin trembling as she speaks.

"I do not want to talk about it right now. We just need to be prepared. We need weapons and make sure that my mom is feeling well enough in case we have to leave."

Julia clutches Crystal's arm, "Crystal you have to tell me!"

"Let's just say that it was so horrible, and if he confronts me; he is the one that will be in some pain."

They grab the jackets and head to Kathy's room. She is dressed and looking better than she has appeared in a long time. They all go downstairs and meet up with Richard in the kitchen. At this point, Richard has the escape routes mapped out with red dotted lines. He walks over to the wet bar and pushes a button under the counter. Suddenly the wall opens up and an array of weapons and survival gear are on display.

"Where did you get all of this?" Julia said.

"I've kept it a secret from everyone, but I am a secret agent for the United States government."

"I knew it!" said Crystal.

Richard starts loading the weapons into the van and hands each of them a gun and ammo. He grabbed a few more gadgets and closes the wall up. "I think we will head up to Big Bear, we have a cabin up there and I am pretty sure he is not aware of it."

"What is this contraption?" Kathy said.

"This is what we call a cell phone, it has not been introduced to the general public since we use it for most of our secret operations." He handed each of them a phone.

"What does it do?" said Julia.

"We will be able to communicate with each other, kind of like a walkie-talkie but better," said Richard.

"How long will it take us to get to Big Bear?" said Crystal.

"About three and half hours," said Richard.

They load up the rest of the gear into the van, lock up the house and head out. "We should probably take Highway I -15 to 18," said Kathy.

"That would be the shortest route," said Richard.

They headed down Interstate 15, it is quiet and not much traffic. They keep a watchful eye, making sure they are not being followed. It is still dark, but the sun should be coming out within an hour. Still no sign of a serial killer trailing behind them, they begin to relax. Now they turn onto Highway 18 and head up to the mountain. The sun breaks through the beautiful Sequoia trees. They turn onto a dirt road that trails back into the mountain; finally reaching the majestic log cabin nestled in a pine tree forest. Small puddles of snow dot the mountainside.

"How long have you owned this cabin?" Julia said. She gazed at the beautiful lodge made out of logs.

"About five years," said Kathy.

"Do you really think we will be safe here, Dad?"

"I sure hope so honey."

They begin the process of unloading the van. Richard unlocks the cabin door and brings in their supplies. He does a walk-through to make sure that they have not been burglarized. "Everything looks secure."

The two-story log cabin is custom-built. It opens up into a large living room and family area. The gourmet kitchen is off to the left. Three bedrooms open off from the family room. A large loft encompasses the upstairs and opens out to a three-sided balcony at the back of the lodge.

Richard goes into stealth mode. He sets up a motion sensor and security lights. Through his monitor, he can view the road coming in and the area behind the cabin. Meanwhile, Crystal starts to load kindling in the fireplace. Kathy heads for the kitchen and begins an inventory of the stock in the cupboards. Julia makes sure there are plenty of blankets to keep them warm.

Everyone is exhausted from their ordeal. Richard agrees to take the first watch while the others get a little sleep. After about four hours, Crystal relieves Richard so he could get some rest. "If you see or hear the slightest thing, come and get me right away," said Richard.

"Don't worry Dad, I will get you 'right away.'"

Richard walks into the master bedroom, he can see the sun shining through the bedroom window which illuminates Kathy's face. He closes the door behind him, which wakes Kathy from her slumber. "Is that you Richard?"

"Yes darling, it is only me." He walks over to the bed and lifts up the blankets to snuggle in next to her.

"I feel so safe with you, I know we are in danger, but it seems so small compared to what I have been through." She holds him close and cups his face with her hands holding him to her chest. They fall asleep in each other's arms.

Richard had not enjoyed a good night's sleep since he lost her. Now laying in her arms, knowing that she is with him; he finally has a good long rest.

He slept for eight hours and then he got up and peeked out the door. He could see that everything was fine and crawled back into bed. Holding her, a warm wave of affection came over him. He stared into her blue eyes and saw the white flax sparkle as she gazed back at him.

Her physical pain gone replaced with a euphoric feeling of delight. No longer was she an invalid on her deathbed. She slowly removed her clothing, smiling with a devilish grin as he gazed at her naked body. That look sent goose bumps up her back. She knew he felt the same way and she loved every minute of it.

He removed his clothing and held her warm body next to his. Desire rose up in him as he began kissing her neck, ears, and making his way to her warm and inviting lips, which slightly parted for him, demanding him to enter.

Soft, slow kisses, turned into deeper more hungry demands until they were both engulfed in desire. It felt like the first time they had actually touched each other, with waves of ecstasy, which never seemed to end. Finally consummating their love in a fiery explosion.

He reclined there in bed, knowing that she is alive and with him once again; he would never let her go. He knew he had cheated fate and it felt good.

Chapter 5

REX MUNDY

REX MUNDY IS FURIOUS. He thinks to himself, *I almost had her, those damn cops.*

The Las Vegas Metropolitan Police Department had their hands full. But they patrolled the area around Richard's home like a magnet in a maze. Covering every inch of the area, but still coming up empty-handed. "Do you see anything, Brian?" Sgt. Johnson asked.

"I got nothing." He lifted his hands up in the air.

"Let's go ahead and end our shift, our relief should be here in about twenty minutes." The patrol car leaves the housing track and heads back to the station.

Meanwhile, Rex has been busy since he was forced to flee the area, he devises a new plan. He had stolen another car, this time a gray Dodge van. He hoped to blend in with the neighborhood since it has a family vehicle look to it.

He is aware that the Nelson's would be on vacation until next week. He pulled the van into the driveway and parked. After studying the neighborhood, he realized that he could go undetected if he sneaked into the backyard.

Originally from Whittier, California, Rex made his way to Las Vegas, Nevada through an unusual route. First his mother, Nancy disappeared after his father brutally beat her. Then he turned his anger on him landing Rex in the hospital of which he suffered a dislocated shoulder, black eye, two broken ribs and a crushed toe.

His aunt Judy, Nancy's sister, arrived at the hospital and took custody of him, nursing his body back to health. It just so happens she lives in Las Vegas.

One night when Judy ended her shift at the Landing Rug Casino, she walked to her car in the covered garage parking lot. There in the darkened corner of the fifth floor stood a man cloaked by the dimness. Tired and slowly moving to her car a man reached through the darkness from behind severing her head from her body. Reynold, Rex's father was always the suspect, but the police had no proof and so the case grew cold. Nancy, Reynold's wife, has never been found.

Feeling deserted by his mother and his aunt, Rex, fell into a deep dark place within his mind.

With no other relatives to raise Rex he was retained in the foster care system.

Rex grew up moving from one foster home, after another. Finally landing with the family who adopted him. The Riley's felt that a stable home would snap Rex out of a troubled childhood. They were murdered for their kindness.

Now on the run, he was able to obtain fake IDs by simply going to the local graveyard and finding someone who is about his age. He would then request their birth certificate. He was quite successful at this and has managed to evade the police for over ten years now.

His photo was on the FBI's most wanted list, which he felt didn't do him any justice. He tried several different disguises over the years and decided that the construction worker is the best look for him. He lied and got a union job which just so happens to be infiltrated by the mob.

That's how he met Jessica, her father, "Jimmy," also known as "The Bull," is a mob, boss. He had gone out with her couple times and she ended up pregnant. Jimmy insisted that they get married, which they did. And then Jimmy started requesting that Rex, start taking out the "trash" for his father-in-law.

Of course, Jessica was unaware of their dirty dealings and murderous behavior. Rex didn't mind too much, he rather enjoyed killing people. He just wanted to decide who would get killed. He has thought about killing Jessica several times, but it wouldn't be much fun for him unless she had blond hair. Besides he needed her to take care of their son Kevin, a rambunctious sort he is, besides if he killed her, then Jimmy would be taking him out like the trash. So there you have it; he was stuck, but he did enjoy murdering on the side.

His dark brown oily hair is in need of a cut, as it hangs down to his shoulders. Pushing his hair out of his face, exposing his dark, deep-set brown eyes with their empty gaze; he stares at Richard's home.

Now he wants Julia, she will be his next victim. First he needs to infiltrate the home. He is clever and has a habit of hiding in his victim's home for days before pouncing on his prey. Going undetected for extended periods of time.

Sneaking into the backyard, he finds the downstairs bathroom window. Taking his Pendleton shirt off; he wraps it around his hand. Carefully hitting the window until the glass breaks. Pulling the loose pieces out of the window until he has cleaned the whole area free from the glass. Slowly, almost like a snake, he creeps through the window until he is well inside.

Opening the bathroom door, he peeks out looking for any sign of life. *The coast is clear.* He walks into the family room, *all is silent.* Then the kitchen, *no signs of life.*

Creeping up the stairs, which slightly creaks on the third step, *still no sound.* He continues walking through the whole house, checking all the rooms. *Dammit, they've escaped, but I think I know where they went.* As he gazes at a picture of Crystal, standing next to a cabin with the caption "Big Bear."

He removes the image from the frame and tucks it into his pocket. Heading downstairs, he stops in the kitchen and opens up the refrigerator. He grabs himself one beer and exits out the back door.

Making his way back to the van, he hops in and takes off. *Big Bear, here I come.*

The new patrol car arrives about five minutes after he left. And has no knowledge of the break-in. Bonnie Brigantine from Channel 8 News shows up. She has been listening to the police scanner and desperately wants more information. She walks over to the police car and asks, "What is going on?"

"It's really nothing, just a family dispute."

"Come on guys give me some information, I know you're looking for the serial killer, I heard it on the scanner."

"No comment, Bonnie."

She walked around the back of the house and spied the broken glass. The back door is wide open. Returning to the front of the house, she rings the doorbell. Finally, she scampers back over to the police car. "Look, guys, the back window of the bathroom is broken and the sliding glass door is wide open," she commented.

The officers exit the police car and make their way to the back yard. Now their guns are drawn. Entering through the back they do a clean sweep of the house. "Clear."

"Clear."

"Better call it in, Paul," said Officer Lieske.

"Jeff. Get the camera rolling," said Bonnie.

"I'm standing here in front of the Clary residence, where a break-in has just occurred. Suspected serial killer Rex Mundy has been seen in the area. I'm advising the citizens in the area to lock your doors and windows until the police can apprehend him."

"Officer Lieske, do you know the whereabouts of the residence?"

"No comment at this time."

"Channel 8 News will continue to investigate and will keep you updated on the events that transpired here today, this is Bonnie Brigantine signing off from Channel 8 News."

"Cut the feed, Jeff."

"Want to get a cup of coffee and regroup?" Jeff asked. As he frowns at Bonnie.

"Yeah let's go over to the Donut House."

They hop in the Channel 8 News van and make their way to the Donut House. They go inside and grab a booth. "This thing is eating you up Bonnie, maybe you shouldn't be reporting this story."

"I can't just give up if it was the other way around my sister would be looking for my killer too!" Her green eyes filling up with tears.

He hated to see her like this. She has always been so full of life and happy most of the time. But since her sister had been murdered three years ago, she didn't seem to have that spark anymore. He gazed at her with his hazel eyes, deeply concerned and quite glad that her hair is reddish-brown instead of a blond. The serial killer had a propensity towards blondes for some reason. Bonnie's sister was blond. As he held her hand, he said, "This guy is dangerous and I'm sure that if your sister were here today she would not want you to put yourself in danger."

"You're probably right, but that's what big sisters do."

"The way I see it; you should let the police do their job."

"Good morning, what would you like for breakfast," said the waitress. As she stood next to them with her pad and pen waiting for their instructions.

"We will take two cups of coffee, and I'll have the glazed donut. What kind of donut would you like Bonnie?"

"I will get a maple bar."

"Okay, I'll be right back with your order."

The waitress gets the order together and brings it back to the table. "Would you like anything else?"

"No, thank you," said Jeff.

After that, they sit quietly eating their donuts and drinking coffee. Bonnie keeps mulling over the information that she has on the killer in her mind, *who is this guy, how many more women are going to die before he's caught? He hates blondes, and he somehow is able to evade the police for so long.*

"I'm going to take you home, I want you to get some rest." He pays the waitress and they get back into the news van. Traveling to her home; all is silent. "Bonnie I can't take much more of this."

"Look I can't let go, I'm sorry." Removing her glasses she holds her head down, rubbing her forehead.

"We are still alive and you need some me time." Glancing at her for a reaction.

"You're right, I just don't know how to turn it off." Smiling up at him, she grabbed his hand and held it in hers. "I love you."

"I love you too, that is why we need to just relax and spend some time just being us. Not the reporter and the camera guy but the man and woman."

"My mind tells me you are right, but my heart aches."

He parked in the driveway, they exit the van. Bonnie pours her body out of the car hanging her shoulders down. Walking like a dead woman she made her way to the door. Jeff followed her. Unlocking the door, he entered resting his keys on the receiving table and grabbed for the phone. He dialed, then waited for the connection.

"Amber, do you and Elizabeth have an opening today?"

"Great, see you in an hour."

Hanging up he glanced at Bonnie, she had already removed her clothes and walked back into the living room in her house coat. "I booked us a couples massage. They will be here in an hour."

"I don't know what I would do without your thoughtfulness." She walks over to him and put her arms around his waist, hugging him tightly as he holds her in his arms.

Jinx, a fluffy white Persian cat, found this opportunity to jump on Jeff's back, digging his nails into his neck as Jeff screams in agony, "Oh!"

"Jinx knock it off!" Grabbing him Bonnie pulls the cat off.

"What is wrong with that cat?"

"I don't know, I think he either wants to participate or maybe he is jealous." She carried him to the kitchen and sat him in front of his dish.

He turned up his nose as if the meal were below him. "Meow."

"I wonder if they will ever catch this guy." She turns and glances at Jeff.

Chapter 6

CAR TROUBLE

REX MANEUVERED THE GRAY van onto the highway. With a full tank of gas, he should make it to Big Bear soon. He continued on Interstate 15 until he reached Highway 18. About a mile past the intersection, he began to have car trouble. Pulling over to the side of the road, he had a mini meltdown. *What the hell do I do now?* His face turns red as his nostrils start to flare. Suddenly he sees a car approaching and regains his composure.

Katie, a college student, has taken a few days off to spend some time with friends up in the mountains. She had the key to her parent's cabin and planned to vacation there a few days. As she made her way up Interstate 18, she could make out a man on the side of the road. His vehicle has broken down. He lifts up his hands and waves to her for help. Being the gentle soul that she is, she stops to give him a lift to the nearest gas station. This would be one of the biggest mistakes she has ever made.

"Hi I'm Katie, are you having some car problems?"

"Yeah, I don't know if it's the fuel pump or what. Do you think you can give me a lift to the nearest gas station?" he said, but his plans were much more devious than that.

"Sure, hop in," reaching over to remove the book and magazines filling the seat.

Rex hops into the gold Thunderbird. "Where are you heading to?" he said, hoping that, it would be a good kill spot. She has long blond hair and blue eyes, which was just his type.

"Just up the road a bit at my parent's cabin," she replied. "What is your name?"

"I'm Ken."

"I need to make a quick stop at the cabin, I need to go to the restroom," she said.

"Yes if you don't mind I need to go too," he replied.

Approaching the cabin Katie can see that her friends have already arrived. And they are standing outside the cabin impatiently. She pulls up front and parks the car. They both get out and head for the group of friends that have mingled at the front door. "Sorry, I'm late, but this guy Ken; has car trouble."

"You're a sucker for a man in need," replied Sebastian, as he studied the fellow, who stood there.

Katie unlocks the door and makes her way to the restroom. Meanwhile, her friends congregate in the living room and start building a blazing fire. When Katie is finished, she motioned her arm to Ken that the bathroom is open.

Rats, I thought I was going to get her alone, dammit. He walks into the restroom.

"You know you shouldn't just pick up a guy on the side of the road. You don't know who he really is," said Sebastian. "I'll take him over to the gas station so he can get some help and you can stay here."

"I agree with Sebastian," said Kim.

"Me too," said Jackie.

"Okay, I'm outnumbered, it probably was kind of a stupid thing to do," said Katie.

The doorbell rings. "That must be Chuck," said Kim. She makes her way to the door to greet her boyfriend.

Rex walks out of the bathroom. He is a little surprised that there is also another guy. *Dammit, this just isn't working out for me at all.*

"Hey Ken, I'll take you to the gas station, it's just up the road," announced Sebastian. He has medium brown hair slightly curly and green eyes. And studies the expression of Ken's face.

They hop in Sebastian's blue Ford truck and drive off. Sebastian gets a very uneasy feeling about the guy. Thankful that the gas station is just up the road a mile. They finally arrive and Rex steps out of the truck. Sebastian waves goodbye and heads back to the cabin.

Rex throws his backpack over his shoulder. He studies the area as he compares it to the picture he has in his pocket. He notices the community mailbox and walks over to inspect the names. *Ha, ha here it is, Clary... The cabin must be up this road.* Rex begins his hike up the path. It took him a lot longer than he expected, but now through the clearing he could see the cabin. And decides to get off the main road and hide in the shelter of the bushes and trees that surround the cottage. He will wait until dark so he can surprise them in their sleep.

Inside the cabin, Crystal decides to turn on the television set. Bonnie Brigantine from Channel 8 News is reporting an incident of the break-in of their home. "Oh my God Julia, that's my house," said Crystal.

"Are you sure?"

"Dad get out here now, I think Rex Mundy has broken into our house," screamed Crystal, as she turned the TV up louder.

Richard grabs his gun and heads for the living room. This was the first time he was thankful for Bonnie Brigantine and her relentless reporting. He watched in horror as, she filmed the broken window and the back door that is wide open; announcing to the world that Rex Mundy is in the area.

"This guy has no fear, he broke into my house even with the cops around," said Richard.

"Do you think he knows about the cabin, Dad?"

"I hope not, but it is a possibility."

"Oh Richard, he's been in our house," said Kathy.

"Look, the worst-case scenario we will just have to time travel," said Richard. "We knew that if we went back in time we were going to have to deal with this Crystal, but we decided that it was worth the risk."

"You're right Dad, we just have to figure out how to get rid of a serial killer. Do we go back in time and try to make sure he is never born? Or do we go forward in time to get away from him?"

"If we go back in time and try to make it so that he's never born, we could change the course of history. Sometimes it's for the best but it could also make things worse," said Richard.

"And if we go forward in time, more people could die," replied Crystal.

"We need to stay together in case we do have to time travel," said Julia.

"Well, whatever we do we better eat something, just in case we have to make a quick getaway," said Kathy, as she began making them a meal for the evening.

They ate their dinner and discussed in depth their options. Each of them making sure that they were dressed and prepared in case they had to make a quick getaway. Because of Richard's extensive background with the government he was able to retrieve information about anyone he chose. So he busily got on his computer and within an hour, he had Rex Munday's place of birth, date and who his parents are.

"I think we should take a chance of going back in time before he was conceived and keep his father and mother from getting together," said Richard.

Julia had stepped outside to take the trash out. The security lights came on, but nobody seemed alarmed since they knew she was taking the trash out. Not until Richard heard his van running.

Rex Mundy grabs Julia around the mouth with a cloth full of chloroform which knocks her out. He tied up her arms and legs and gagged her mouth. Then he threw her into Richards van. Being an expert in cars, he hot-wires it. And sped off down the dirt road.

Richard is in shock and feeling foolish. First he starts to chase the vehicle knowing he's no match for the speeding van. But then the thought comes into his mind. He goes back inside the cabin and they huddle next to each other. "Okay, this is what we are going to do, we're going to go back in time maybe twenty minutes before this happened, and were not going to let Julia go outside."

"Okay, here goes," said Crystal, as they huddle together and Richard sets the *Sphere* for twenty minutes earlier. And like clockwork they transfigured to twenty minutes earlier.

"Wow, that's just absolutely crazy," said Kathy, still feeling a little dizzy from the transition.

"What do you mean?" Julia asked.

"Julia, don't go outside to take out the trash, Rex Mundy's out there," said Crystal.

"Okay, were all together and we are going back in time to Whittier, California," said Richard, as they huddle together, they transfigure to 1951.

"Wow, I could really get used to this!" Julia said. "I think we are next to a dairy farm."

"Yes, Rex Mundy's father, works here," said Richard.

The Sanderson dairy farm has been in operation for twenty years. Situated just next to Bora Avenue. Quite a well-established farm, the dairy building was large with fifty milking stalls. Of course, the building is painted white which was the standard for any dairy farm and it was accented with red trim. The fifty- acre ranch consisted of alfalfa fields along with a bountiful orange grove.

"Okay, this is my plan, first I will get a job at his dairy farm and get as close to Reynold Mundy as I can," said Richard.

"What do you want me to do?" Kathy asked.

"According to my research there should be a house for rent on Bora Street can you see it over there?"

"Yes, I see it, the brown one with the sign outside."

"Here's some money I want you to go over there and talk to them and rent that house and you girls can get settled in. Then when I find out where Rex's mother lives I want you to make friends with her. When she starts talking about Reynold, I want you to influence her into believing that he is a dangerous man. But we will have plenty of time to figure all that out for now, I just want you, girls, to get settled in and I'll meet you back over there as soon as possible."

"Honey, I love you; be careful," said Kathy.

"Okay Dad, will see you then," said Crystal.

Richard walks up the winding dirt road which leads up to the dairy house. The orange grove is in blossom and the beautiful fragrance lingers in the air. This also helps mask the smell of manure piles along the way. Richard couldn't help but think, *how such a peaceful place could be the beginning of something so horrifying, I just don't get it.*

He raps on the door and then waits for any sign of life. Finally, after no one answers, he walks over to the dairy stalls. A tall, thin man with curly light brown hair and green eyes walks over to greet him.

"Hello, can I help you?" the man says.

"Hi, my name is Richard Clary, I was hoping that you have a job opening," extending his arm out; he shakes his hand.

"Yes actually I am looking for someone, can you start right away?"

"Sure."

"My name is Reynold Mundy, the job here is quite straightforward, but it is time-consuming."

"I can handle that," looking at Reynold directly in the eye.

"This here contraption is for milking the cows, it must be put on securely like this. They also need to be fed and I have a schedule up here that shows you what times to feed them."

"Okay, I can do that I helped my uncle on his farm."

"Under no circumstances are you to go in the building at the back of the house. That building is off-limits," he crossed his arms.

"Okay."

"On Fridays I go to the auction, sometimes you'll have to come with me to help load up some cattle."

"It pays one-hundred dollars a week and you get Saturday and Sunday off."

"Great."

"I'm actually getting ready to go to the auction and I could really use some help today. So if you can start today, I will be leaving in about twenty minutes."

"No problem, do you need me to do anything?"

"Yes if you could load up some of that alfalfa in the trailer, we can get on our way."

Richard charges the alfalfa into the back of the trailer. He can't believe his luck, getting the job right away. He thinks *I wonder what he's hiding in that building behind the house? I'll have to find a way to get back there when he's not around.*

They both climb into the truck and haul the trailer down to the auction. Along the way, they strike up a conversation. "So where you from Richard?"

"I'm actually from Utah."

"And how about you?"

"I actually have lived in Whittier all my life."

"Are you married?"

"Not yet, there's this lady named Nancy that I've seen for a while."

"How about you?"

"Yeah, I've been married for a while now. Her name is Kathy."

"Well, here we are, we can just leave the trailer here. The auction house should be open for bids in about five minutes or so."

They walk over to the bidding section. Reynold studies the cattle, checking for any diseases. The auction house is full. It consisted of an indoor arena with the auctioneer sitting up high on the platform.

"Do I hear five-thousand, do I hear five- thousand and fifty, five-thousand and fifty-five... sold to Jackson."

"Now we have a beautiful specimen of milking cows to start off bidding with five-thousand, five-thousand, five-thousand.... sold to Reynold."

"Okay, Richard, load them up."

Richard starts loading up the cattle onto the trailer. Meanwhile, Reynold speaks to a petite looking woman with brown hair and brown eyes. She looks to be about twenty-five years old wearing a tan sweater with a green emerald brooch and light green pants. Her hair is done up in a beehive style something that Richard hadn't seen in a long time. She has a pleasant smile too. Richard wondered, *is that Nancy, Rex's mom?*

"Hey, darling, how about I pick you up at seven?" Reynold said. As he moved closer to erase the distance between them.

"I will see you then," she replied, reaching up to kiss him on the lips.

They said their goodbyes and Reynold proceeded to help Richard load the cattle. They have picked up some beautiful looking Holstein cows with large black and white spots all over their body, these dairy cattle are quite famous for producing large quantities of low-fat milk.

"I made out today," said Reynold, lifting his chin high and exposing his neck.

"Those are some beautiful looking Holstein cows," replied Richard, as he patted one of the cows with his hand.

Finishing their task they proceeded back to the farm. The way home was quiet and Richard kept wondering how he could influence the situation. He wanted to keep these two apart as long as he could, but he needed a plan. If that is Nancy, they should not get together tonight or any night. And he started thinking, *I will sneak back over and let the cattle out, it should take him some time to round them back up, hopefully, that will detain his date.*

Arriving back at the farm, they unloaded the cattle. The sun was beginning to set and the sky burst forth with beautiful streaks of purple and pink.

"Okay Richard, I will meet you back here Monday morning; how about 5:00 A.M.?"

"I will be here," he smiled as he walked away.

Richard headed down the winding dirt road. Stopping halfway through the orange grove, he cut back over to the cattle stable. Unlatching the gate and swooshing the cattle out. Once he had completed his mission, he headed back through the grove and continued until he reached the rental house.

"Here comes Dad," said Crystal, as she opens up the door and let him in. "How did it go, Dad?"

"Well, I got a job with Reynold and he took me over to the auction and I think that I saw the serial killer's mom. He is supposed to go out on a date with her tonight, but I went back over to the stable when he was not looking and unlatched the gate. I am hoping that will keep him busy; trying to round up the cattle. I do not think they will be going out tonight."

"What was she like?" Julia asked.

"Actually she is a petite woman, kind of attractive and seemed very pleasant. I have a hard time wrapping my mind around this," said Richard. "I guess I actually imagined in my mind that she would have to be this horrible woman to have this kid but, I am not getting that at all."

"What about Reynold what is he like?" Kathy asked.

"So far he has been nice but he did say something a little strange. There is one building on the property that he said is off-limits. He does not want me to go in there."

"What do you think is in there, Richard?

"I do not know, but I will have to find out."

Meanwhile back on the dairy farm, Reynold is trying desperately to round up the cattle. *How in the hell did the cattle get out?* He thought to himself. It took him about two hours to get all the cattle back into the stables.

He called Nancy on the phone. "Nancy, darling we will have to make plans for tomorrow night instead. The cows got out and I had to round them up."

"How in the world did that happen?" she replied.

"I do not know. I have this new guy; maybe he just did not latch it properly."

"I wish I could have seen you running around chasing cattle," as she giggled at the thought of it.

"Hilarious," he replied.

"I will pick you up tomorrow at 7:00 P.M. and I will take you out to eat and then we will go to a movie, okay?"

"Okay, I will see you tomorrow, bye."

Chapter 7

WHITTIER RENTAL

KATHY RAPS ON THE rental house door. Crystal and Julia stroll around the perimeter of the property, examining the workmanship and inspecting the neighbor's car. A sleek black Hudson with a tan side scoop is parked next door. Neither one of them has ever seen anything like it.

"Wow, what a cool looking car," said Crystal.

"No kidding, sensational," replied Julia.

A little old lady about seventy-five years old opens the creaky front door. "Are you here about the house?" said the woman.

"Yes, I was hoping it was available right away. My name is Kathy Clary and these are my daughters, Crystal, and Julia."

"It is nice to meet you. My name is Burrell and the house is available today, for the right price."

"Will this do?" Kathy said, holding out a handful of money.

"That should take care of you for five months. Come on in, this is a living room and it has four bedrooms and an enormous kitchen and two baths. Electric is included in the rent. It is fully furnished, in magnificent shape and I expect it to be returned to me, in the same condition that I left it."

"Great then I will just pay in advance for five months."

"Okay, here are the keys and if you have any problems, I live next-door."

Burrell scurried off, although she is older she sports a dark red hair color with a touch of gray at the roots signaling it was time for a touch up. Kathy could finally relax. She is a little nervous about her new surroundings, but she has finished her assignment.

"I think I could really get used to this time travel, I find it really intriguing all the different styles and different kinds of cars it's better than a history lesson," said Crystal.

"I know what you mean, it feels surreal like I am on a movie set. Even the air seems lighter," replied Julia.

Clary Cabin

Meanwhile, back in time, Rex is hiding outside of the Clary cabin. He decides to wait until nightfall, then he will make his move. He has not seen any movement in the cabin for a few hours. He creeps up to the cabin and the security lights come on. Still he sees no change.

He finds a blind spot to the security lights and creeps underneath. Resting his body against the wall of the cabin, he inches his way along the wall. Finally, he reaches the steps to the back balcony and slithers up the stairs like a snake. He reaches the back door to the second floor. He pulls out his lock-picking kit. And in about two movements he has the back door open.

Still he encounters no one. He peeks over the balcony down to the first floor. He can see monitors set up and he goes downstairs to investigate. The lights are still on in the kitchen and fire is blazing in the fireplace. He thinks to himself, *there must be someone here.* But as he continues to investigate it becomes increasingly apparent that no one is in the cabin except for him.

I do not get it, he thought to himself. *The van is still here, fire is going, where could they have gone?* He decides to take advantage of the situation.

First he gets himself something to eat then he starts checking the cabin for any belongings that could be useful to him.

His mind begins to wander off thinking about that other girl just down the road. He decides he can hotwire the van and if he cannot have Julia, then he will just have to settle for Katie, for now.

He throws his backpack over his shoulder, carrying a few extra items that he did not have before. Hot wiring the van, he is now in the business. And he makes his way down the path. He finds a back road which follows along behind Katie's cabin. Parking the van; he waits.

Inside the cabin, Katie and Sebastian are getting cozy on the couch as they play a game of backgammon. Warmed by the fire blazing away in the fireplace and Chardonnay in their glasses.

"You beat me again, Katie!" Sebastian said, as he grabbed her and cuddled her tightly.

"You are losing on purpose, I know you are," she replied, kissing him on the nose.

"I am just not good at this game," he replied, holding up his hands, acting all innocent.

Chuck starts laughing, "Ha, ha, ha you guys are too funny." His burly laugh fits his physique impeccably. Pushing his medium length, dark blond hair away from his face; exposing his round peachy cheeks and his blue eyes. He puts his arm around Kim's neck and holds her a little tighter.

She smiles at Chuck and gives him a big kiss. "You are such a cutie," said Kim, as she gazes up into his eyes.

"I am a guy, and guys are not cute they're handsome. Now you, on the other hand; with that curly purple hair and big blue eyes and a rocking body, are cute."

"Are you guys stoned?" Katie asked as she examined their red eyes.

"I hope so. Otherwise the guy who gave me this joint is going to get it," replied Chuck. "Ha, ha, ha."

"Come on honey, let's go upstairs," said Kim, as she leads him to the guest bedroom.

Once inside the bedchamber Kim dims the lights and turns on the stereo. Music could be heard in the background. She begins to do a striptease for him. And sings out loud a song, "Only you can keep me going all night. " Uncovering her shoulders slowly, she turns around to face him and she drops her silky pink blouse. She motions to him with her index finger and then places it on her lips.

Chuck's eyes zero in on her exposed breasts and he begins to take his clothes off exceedingly fast. He lifts her up into his arms as she straddles her legs around his waist and they fall into bed together.

Rex is glaring at them through the window, waiting for his opportunity to pounce on his victim. *Are these guys ever going to go to sleep?* He thinks to himself.

Meanwhile, Jackie and her boyfriend Mike return to the cabin after a beer run. Jackie is the perky type, full of energy. She has brown eyes and light brown hair, which is about shoulder length. Her hair is layered and she always has it curled. Mike, on the other hand, has short black hair and brown eyes. He has a bodybuilder physique. "Well, we got some more beer and I got you another bottle of Chardonnay," Mike said.

"Just in time I just ran out," said Katie.

"Where are Kim and Chuck?" Jackie asked.

"Oh, I think they're having a private party in the bedroom," said Sebastian. "If you know what I mean."

"Now that sounds like a plan," said Mike, he turns to Jackie and smiles. She grins.

"Did you pick up some hamburger patties and buns like I asked you?" said Katie.

"Of course I did I'm starving," said Mike.

Mike and Sebastian go out to the back patio and start up the barbecue. Meanwhile, Katie and Jackie begin the process of slicing up onions, tomatoes, and lettuce. Both of them grab another glass of Chardonnay. They snack on the chips while they wait.

Finally, the briquettes are ready. Katie takes the hamburger patties out to the barbecue and places them on the grill. She takes the opportunity to sneak in a cigarette without Sebastian seeing her.

Rex Spies her through the bushes. He pulls out a bottle from his jacket, he unscrews the cap of the chloroform and places the cloth over the opening, saturating it. He reaches out from the bushes and covers her mouth tightly and holds her until she passes out. He drags her body to the van and ties her up. Then he speeds off down the road. *Finally,* he thinks, *I have her alone.*

An old abandoned warehouse on the outskirts of Las Vegas has been his kill spot for a few years now. He knows he won't be disturbed there. Jimmy, also known as "The Bull" uses it occasionally for money-laundering. But Rex knows he doesn't have any business there for at least another month. Rex has been using the basement to do his business.

Sebastian walks out to the back patio and he doesn't see Katie anywhere. He steps back inside the cabin. "Hey, have you guys seen Katie, I thought she was barbecuing the hamburgers?"

Jackie steps outside to the back patio and notices that the hamburgers are aflame. "Sebastian the hamburgers are burning!"

Sebastian and Jackie start removing the burgers. After that, Sebastian walks to the side of the cabin and notices a cigarette butt that is still lingering with smoke. "Katie where are you? I know you're out here I found your cigarette butt. You know you shouldn't be smoking."

But there is no response. He walks around the perimeter of the cabin, still no sign of Katie. He does find some drag marks and becomes alarmed. He follows the drag marks that lead to a dirt road. And he can see a van driving off in the distance. "Holy shit!" he screams.

He runs back to the cabin and tells Jackie, "Call the police they need to be on the lookout for a burnt orange van. Someone just took Katie."

Jackie calls the police, then she goes to the guest room and gets Kim and Chuck. Meanwhile, Mike and Sebastian jump in Katie's gold Thunderbird and haul buns down the road, chasing after the van.

Chuck secures the windows and doors and waits for the police to arrive. The girls are shaken up and he can't seem to calm them down.

Mike and Sebastian are quite a distance behind him, but they are making good time. Rex hadn't noticed them at all, as he continued to drive. Finally, he pulls the van into the abandoned warehouse. Then he drags her body down into the basement and chains her up.

The sick, deranged man is pleased with his capture. His excitement is escalating. Down in the dark dungeon of the basement he unleashes his madness. Taking his sharp serrated hunting knife, he proceeds to cut the blouse from Kim's body, one by one the buttons fall, savoring every moment on his camera; which is set up in the corner.

Reflecting back to previous victims as he studies the jewelry he has stored in a cedar box. He removes Katie's pukka shell necklace and replaces it with a black leather leash. Still unconscious from the chloroform, she doesn't flinch. Then he straps and object made of a red ball and black leather that harnesses over her head and mouth.

He positions her body over a metal contraption that resembles a jungle gym and chains her to it. He rolls out a leather organizer on the table, containing different torturing tools which resemble a hospital operating room setup.

He turned on the television, he pops in the VHS tape, which begins to play a video of a woman who's being tortured. The victim on the video is tortured by him. Screams and crying fill the room and he becomes extremely excited.

Still unconscious from the chloroform, he positions himself from behind her and repeatedly violates her to his animalistic satisfaction.

Sebastian and Mike enter the abandoned warehouse. They find the van but not Katie. Mike reaches down and picks up a metal rod found lying on the garage floor. Meanwhile, Sebastian finds a rake hanging on the wall. Mike motions to the door leading to the basement.

Because of his deranged excitement and the screaming coming from the video, Rex does not see or hear Sebastian and Mike enter the basement. He continues his hedonistic behavior until Mike raises the shaft and bashes him over the head with a metal rod. He falls to the floor unconscious while Sebastian finds the keys to the locks which enslave his beloved. Tears glisten from the corner of his eyes as he removes the harness from her face and chains from her arms and legs.

He covers her body with a blanket. "She's still alive, but unconscious," said Sebastian.

Mike takes the chains that enslaved Katie and applies them to Rex. "He won't get out of this."

Sebastian turns off the video recorder. The room falls silent and Sebastian turns towards Mike, both of them shake their head in disbelief, "What a sick bastard!" Sebastian said.

"I will stay here with this piece of shit while you take her to the hospital, and send the police to this address," said Mike.

"Alright buddy, I'll get them here as soon as I can."

Sebastian gathers Katie into his arms and carries her out of the basement up the stairs. He puts her in the car and heads to the hospital.

Once he arrives at Sun Valley hospital, they immediately take care of her in the emergency room. It's touch and go for about four hours. He informs the police of the location of the abandoned warehouse where Mike is still waiting; watching the lunatic.

The Las Vegas Metropolitan Police Department is dispatched to the abandoned warehouse. Upon their arrival, they encircle the building and slowly maneuver inside. The officers rest on the wall of the stairwell and ease their way down into the basement.

Mike can hear them coming down and yells out, "I've got him over here; he's chained up."

"Sir, I need you to back away from the perpetrator," said Officer Jackson.

"No problem, I'm glad you are here."

Officers make their way; surrounding Rex until they feel that the building is clear and there are no other killers. They examine the room and discover the monsters tools. The evidence department enters the basement and starts logging and tagging each and every item, photographing all of the evidence as they shake their heads in disbelief. While the police officers handcuff and shackle Rex and prepare to load him into a paddy wagon. He does the chained feet shuffle toward the vehicle leaning to one side, a clear indication of a head wound; maybe brain damage.

Right in front of their eyes he begins to disappear until the shackles and handcuffs literally drop to the ground. "Am I losing my mind or did the guy just vanish into thin air?" Officer Jackson said.

"What the hell?" replied Officer Kennedy as he stared with bewilderment?

All of a sudden, everything starts to go in reverse. And the remnants that Rex was ever alive disappears. Katie is standing outside having a cigarette on the side of the house by the bushes. She puts out her cigarette and returns to the hamburger patties on the grill. She flips them and then Sebastian walks out to kiss her.

"Katie, I thought I told you not to smoke; it's atrocious for you and it tastes horrible."

"I'm trying honey; I am going to quit."

Chapter 8

WHAT IS NEXT

KATHY HAD DINNER ON the table when Richard arrived home. She and the girls had gone grocery shopping earlier that day. They were amazed at the low cost of their grocery items. They have no idea how long they would be there, so Kathy bought enough groceries for a couple of days. The price of the porterhouse steak is so cheap she could not resist. She also checked out the produce section and put a beautiful salad together.

Richard continued to explain the events of his day. He kept thinking in his mind, *I really need to find out what is inside the building on the back of the house.*

After dinner, they all decided to sit out on the front porch. The house is one of the old-fashioned homes where they still have the covered front porch so you can rock in your chair and listen to the children playing in the neighborhood. It is a simpler time. Richard almost didn't want to go back to the future. He enjoyed the quiet, relaxed atmosphere; it reminded him of his childhood. But he had a responsibility to his family and to their new way of life. Oh, they could go on these excursions and hopefully improve things that are going wrong in the world but he needed to stay grounded. He needed to stay focused on his reason for being there in the first place. He knew that if this works; his life and the lives of his family and Julia would never be the same again.

Crystal and Julia walk inside and sit down at the dining table. Crystal pulled out a deck of cards. Sitting across from each other, they realize just how lucky they are. Crystal smiles thinking about how wonderful it is to have her friend Julia back, alive and something as simple as playing a card game. Her mother healthy and active gives her a feeling that is not easy to put into words; *gratitude.*

Julia is so happy to see that Crystal is not sad anymore. Her mother being alive brought that sparkle back in her eyes.

They all decided to retire for the evening. Excited and a little exhausted, they fell fast asleep. Probably the best night sleep that, they all had in a very long time.

The next morning Richard was up very early. He already combed through the phone book and found Nancy's address and phone number. Peering out the side window of the house, he saw a "for sale" sign on the black Hudson next-door. The price was extremely reasonable so he decided to go next door and check it out.

He knocked on Burrell's door and waited for an answer. Finally, Burrell opens the door. "Hi you must be Richard," said Burrell.

"Yes, and you must be Burrell," he replied.

"Is everything working out okay with the house?"

"Yes, everything is fine," he replied. "I noticed that you have this car for sale and I would like to buy it," he studied the older woman's face; waiting for an answer.

"I really can't drive anymore so I thought that I would sell it," she steps back into the house; picks up the keys and the title. Richard follows Burrell inside the house. "My granddaughter Violet disappeared about two years ago, she used to drive me around to run my errands, but since her disappearance I've been on my own."

"Is this a picture of Violet?" Richard asked, picking up a photo of a young woman on the fireplace mantle. He studies the portrait searching for signs or clues but finds none.

"Yes, that is my precious Violet," as she reflected back on her granddaughter's beautiful blue eyes that sparkled and shined with such delight. Her long flowing blond hair that framed her face and cascaded down her back is etched in Burrell's memory. Such a sweet innocent girl with her whole life ahead of her. *What could have happened to her?*

"I'm sorry to hear about your unfortunate situation with Violet," he said. "Do the police have any leads?"

"Not that I'm aware of," she said, as sadness flushed over Burrell's face.

"How does this car run, is it in good shape?"

"Yes, she runs like a dream." *Burrell reflects back to an earlier time when she and Violet would go on joy rides through the country.*

"Here's the money for the car and if you ever need a ride to the store or anything just let me know; I would be glad to help you out any way I can."

"I appreciate that and I may have to take you up on that offer."

"Like I said, it's no problem."

Dungeon

Inside the damp, dark, musty room; the whimpering of a young woman can be heard. The sound of a creaking door opens and the light shines through into the interior; exposing a young girl who is chained up. Her once white sundress is now smudged with dirt, torn and tattered. Violet's sunken, dim, blue eyes never gazed up, fixed on the filthy floor. Her turned down mouth, along with the thin, frail arms and legs resembled the commercials about starving beaten dogs seen on the nightly programming. Receiving only one meal a day she has become malnourished. He doesn't care, she's only there for one reason; his enjoyment.

She tries not to look directly into his eyes; knowing that if she does he may actually hurt her again. She must conserve as much energy as she can. Maybe that way she will have a chance of surviving. He lays a plate of food down next to her. And as quickly as he entered the room; he leaves.

She scrounged for the little bit of food left behind for her; hoping that he will not return. *If I can just survive another day.*

He exits the building from behind the house and heads to the corral to feed the milking cows. His cowboy boots are dirty and his hands are covered with gloves, as he continues to feed the rest of the livestock. To him, it's just another day.

Back at the house, Richard said, "I have good news, I just bought the car next-door."

"What's our next plan?" Kathy asked.

"I have Nancy's address and I think we will just drive over there and stakeout her place," replied Richard.

They load up into the car and head to the address. Once they arrive, they sit and wait. Nancy walks out of her house and gets into her car. They follow her to a dress shop. She gets out of the car and goes inside. After about an hour, she is still inside. "Maybe she works here," Crystal said.

"Yeah, you're probably right. Why don't you guys go inside and look around and find out if she does."

Kathy, Crystal, and Julia go inside the dress shop. They browsed around looking at dresses and other clothing items and periodically scanning the room. Nancy is, in fact, working at the counter. They strike up a conversation with her. Noticing that she's wearing an emerald brooch with the beautiful black dress. The brooch is so unusual that it actually captured their attention. And the funny thing is Crystal noticed that it looks like it is from the emerald necklace that she has. The chain actually had one jewel missing from the back of the string, which has a striking resemblance to the brooch Nancy is wearing? She kept it in the back of her mind. She made a mental thought about it and then proceeded to carry on a conversation. "I really like the dress that you have on, did you purchase it here?"

"Yes it's from our fall collection," she replied.

"Do you think you might have that in my size?"

"I believe that we might have two left and there might be one in your measurement, let's have a look over here."

"I can't help but admire your emerald brooch, is that a family heirloom?"

"I actually received this from my mother, and it has been handed down from generation to generation." Her hand slowly removes the black dress from the rack, "I think you might be a size six, so this should work. I will set you up a room."

Crystal follows Nancy to the dressing room. Nancy hangs the dress up on the hook. "I will return and check on you," she said, and then she walked away to help the other customers.

"We're new in town and I was wondering if you knew of any nice places to go out to; on a Saturday night?" Kathy asked.

"We have an excellent drive-in theater off of Washington Boulevard; my boyfriend and I like to go there."

"Oh, that sounds fantastic, we haven't been to a drive-in, in a very long time."

"We're going there tonight to see a double-feature," Nancy replied.

"Do you know the name of the movie playing?"

"Oh yes, *A Streetcar Named Desire* with Marlon Brando and Vivien Leigh," Nancy's eyes gaze up at the ceiling as if she was in a dream state.

"How do I look, Mom?" Crystal asked, as she twirled and moved around the room in a black dress, elegantly showing the front and then the back, batting her eyelashes as she showed off. Finally, doing a curtsy and looking up at her mother. Something that she had missed when her mother had been gone for so long.

"Crystal, that dress looks gorgeous on you," replied her mother, as she looked at Crystal and then back at Nancy.

"That dress really is stunning on you, do you need a pair shoes to match?" Nancy turned her attention to the mother wondering if she was going to get a bigger sell out of this.

"Oh Mom, can I get shoes to go with it?" her eyes gaze up at her mom, waiting patiently for her answer.

"Okay; yes, you will need a pair shoes to match the dress." Kathy examines the inside of her purse, looking for her wallet to make sure she has enough money.

Nancy escorts Crystal to the shoe section, as they mull over the different styles, selecting a pair of black high heels to match. The phone rings and Nancy walked over to the counter to answer it. While she is on the phone, they eavesdrop on the conversation. Once Nancy gets off the phone, Kathy asked, "Is that your boyfriend?"

"Yes, Reynold wants to take me to a restaurant before we go to the movies."

"That wouldn't be Reynold Munday; would it?" said Julia.

"Why yes," she replied. She looked fixedly with wide open eyes at the young girl wondering what she meant by that.

Julia tried not to make eye contact as she gazed down at the floor with her hands behind her back. Rubbing her foot on the floor in front of her. Then she slowly looked up at Nancy and said, "I don't think you should go out with him. My neighbor down the street said that he could be quite violent; if he doesn't get his way."

"What do you mean, what did she say?" replied Nancy.

"Well, she said that she went out with him and he got a little frisky; she told him no, and then he got infuriated and he slapped her."

"I've never seen that side of him," she pondered her mind as she looked for clues in the past but finding none.

"What's the name of that theater again," said Kathy.

"Sundown Drive-in Theater on Washington Boulevard," she replied, slowly she picked up the garments and brought them up to the register. Then in silence she rang up their items. Deep in thought, she stared at the counter then back to the register as she rang up the items.

"Thank you, Nancy," said Kathy, picking up her packages they exited the building.

"I think it worked."

"Wow, I believe you over did it, Julia," said Crystal.

"No, I don't think she overdid it; I think it was perfect," replied Kathy.

Warped Chapter 9

VIOLET SURPRISE

THE SUN WAS BEGINNING to set in the sleepy town of Whittier. Reynold prepares to go on his date with Nancy. He pulls out a small box from his coat pocket opening it one more time. The ring glistens with the light in the kitchen. He would ask her to marry him tonight. Oh, of course, he would have to hide his extracurricular activities which would be a slight inconvenience. But he did need help around the house and she was pleasant enough. *Maybe I could buy the Dell Ranch it is only three miles away and I could store my ladies there.* Continuing to secure the building and lock everything up, he heads out to pick up Nancy.

Richard sees his chance as he watches Reynold's car drive down the road out of sight. Richard walks through the orange grove and cuts over to the house. Going from the house to the building that he has been told to stay out of; he begins to inspect the lock. Finally, he discovers the corner on the back of the building that has come loose. He grabs a crowbar from the garage and begins to meticulously pull back the planks of the wood until there was enough room for him to crawl in.

Turning on his flashlight, he discovers a woman huddled in the corner and in fear for her life.

"Don't worry miss, I'm actually here to help you," he approaches her and takes the crowbar and twists until he's able to break the chain.

Hysterically, she huddles in the corner, "You must hurry he will be back any minute!" she said. "He always comes back!"

Just as they begin to climb out of the back of the building, Reynold ushers Violet and Richard back in and hammers shut the planks. The hammer banged against the wood; reverberating. Violet clings to Richard in total fear. He lifts his foot and kicks at the planks, but it is useless they will not budge.

Reynold unlocks the front of the building carrying a massive hammer. "You just couldn't leave things alone could you, Richard? I told you to stay out of this building and now look at the mess you have put me in; now I have to do something with you."

He lunges at Richard; narrowly missing his head by two inches with the hammer as Richard ducks. The vigorous force caused by the weight of the hammer launches Reynold forward in which he slips and falls. Richard jumps on top of him freeing the weapon from his hand. They continue rolling back and forth, first Reynold has an upper hand than Richard. He clocks Reynold in the face but just misses and hits his ear slamming his fist to the ground.

Reynold rolls him off, pulls Richard to his feet and hits him square in the face. He falls to the ground, trying to get back up, but Reynold kicks him in the gut. He grabs his stomach in agony. Reynold climbs on top of him grabs Richard's hair on both sides of his head and starts banging his cranium on the cement until; he loses consciousness.

Violet huddles in a corner weeping. She stands up and tries to make a run for the door. But it's useless he reaches for her, grabs her, sliding her body on the ground like a sack of potatoes and locks her up one more time in her chains. He gags her mouth and then he proceeds to chain up Richard and covers his mouth with a rag. "I will take care of you; later! I have a date and you are not going to ruin it!"

Whittier House

"He is not back yet, something must have gone wrong. I'll wait another fifteen minutes and then we better go investigate," said Crystal.

Crystal paced back and forth in the kitchen as she rubs the back of her neck and then crosses her arms over her chest; wondering if they had made a mistake.

Wrinkling her eyebrow while biting her lip. "I cannot take it anymore; you girls stay here if I am not back in fifteen minutes you go over to Burrell's and call the police; got it?" said Kathy.

"Okay Mom, but we are only going to wait fifteen minutes," as she takes a deep breath to calm herself.

Kathy rushes through the orange grove and cuts over to the back building.

"I think it's been ten minutes I just can't wait anymore, Crystal let's just go over to Burrell's and call the police," as she clasped her hands together.

Crystal and Julia go over to Burrell's house and get on the phone and call the cops.

The Dairy Farm…

Kathy stands outside of the building behind the house, desperately is trying to unlock the door. Rubbing her hands on her pant legs attempting to keep them dry so she could continue to pull on the lock. Inside she could hear Richard and Violet screaming out, "We're in here, we're in here!" Although they are muffled sounds.

She goes into the garage and grabs the hammer. Returning to the lock, she smashes the hammer onto the padlock repeatedly. Kathy could hear the sirens moving closer to the house, she spotted the flashing lights, the police are in view.

The Whittier Police Department is on the scene within five minutes. The police cut the lock with a bolt cutter. Inside they remove the chains and free them from their prison. Kathy holds Richard in her arms. The ambulance arrives and they start doctoring up Richard's head, they are concerned that he may have a slight concussion, but they say he'll be okay. They load them into the van.

Violet, on the other hand, is profoundly malnourished and needs urgent medical care. Burrell arrives clinging to her not wanting to leave her side. Happy that her granddaughter is alive, she continues to kiss her on the forehead. She thanked Richard for saving her Violet. She hops into the ambulance along with Crystal, Julia, and Kathy.

"You need to get to the movie theater right away. He has a young woman named Nancy with him," Richard cried out.

"Send the troopers to Sundown Drive-in theater right away," Officer Freeman broadcasts over the radio.

Continuing their investigation they find ten bodies buried in the ground behind the building. The missing women of Whittier have been found, unfortunately not alive. It was the most gruesome sight the WPD has ever seen.

The Date….

Reynold arrives at Nancy's house and picks her up for their date. It is surprising that he showed no signs of any distress. "Darling I think I'll take you to "Sammy's Grill," they have an incredible country skillet. I think you might enjoy it. The meal has an apple, sausage, and mushrooms. They add onions in a scrambled egg cheese dish with some potatoes. They usually serve it with a muffin, how does that sound?"

"Absolutely delicious, you know exactly what I like," she replied.

They arrive at the restaurant, which is nice and cozy. Enjoying their meal; Reynold kept smiling at her. She kept thinking about what had happened earlier. And she just couldn't believe it when she looked at his face, he is so sweet to her there is no way he possibly could be the guy that that girl was talking about. Finally, they finished dinner and headed on to the theater.

Pulling into the Sundown Drive-in theater, she felt so relaxed. She could really get used to having her life with Reynold. They smiled at each other and went to the concession stand to purchase some popcorn and sodas and then headed back to their vehicle.

The movie was about to begin and Reynold smiles at Nancy and then he pulls out a little box from his pocket. He opened up the case and he turned to Nancy. "Darling will you marry me?"

"Oh honey, of course, I'll marry you," she smiles at him relaxing her posture her eyes shining her lips part as she softly kissed him.

He takes the ring out of the box and places it on her finger and then they cuddle up next to each other as the movie begins. Lost in a dream state of just the two of them. Nancy, feeling a little lightheaded from all the excitement and a little shiver of pleasure, a tingle throughout her body.

As the movie progresses, Blanche Dubois's is an attractive southern belle whose pretense of the virtue and manners thinly masked her alcoholic and delusional grandeur. She heads off for her sisters' who live in New Orleans. She is told to go and take a streetcar named desire to transfer to cemeteries and then ride a six blocks and get off at Elysium Fields. At which point she is stunned by the steamy urban ambiance which is a shock to Blanche's nerves.

Unfortunately right at that moment the police surround Reynold's car. "Step out of the car sir; with your hands up!"

Reynold raises his hands above his head. He thought *I have to make a run for it.*

Nancy is in complete shock stunned by the fear of guns drew and police standing all around the car. Slowly the police officer opens up the door, at which point Reynold shoves the door, knocking the officer down and makes a run for it. The police are chasing him. He pulls a gun out of his pocket, turns to shoot but before he can get one shot off, he is gunned down. Laying in a pool of blood, Nancy can only look on in horror.

Nancy fell into hysteria, outbursts of unmanageable sobs poured forth like an uncontrollable river heading downstream with no end.

"You are safe now ma'am, we got the serial killer," he placed his arm around her shoulder.

Nancy thinks, *How could I be so wrong, how could I not see that there was something wrong with him.* That is a question that will haunt her for the rest of her life. A moment that was supposed to be so beautiful and happy had turned into the most horrible experience of her life.

"Come with me ma'am," said the officer, as he guided her to the ambulance truck.

The police tried to talk to her, but the shock is too much. The medic gave her something to relax her. She began to doze off and fell into a nightmare. Waking quite abruptly. Now she is riding in the ambulance to the hospital.

Reynold's body is loaded into another truck. The automobile pulls out of the theater. Men walk back and forth announcing that the theater has to close early due to their investigation. Patrons scurry from the parking spots looking on as they drive pass, wondering why. Before, a lively event has now grown silent.

The swings sit unmoved and silent in the darkness like a ghost.

Gun shells are tagged and bagged. Chalk is drawn on the site of the body where a pool of blood still lingers.

Everyone knew the drive-in theater would never be the same again. Once a lively place where family, lovers, and friends gathered for an evening of fun and entertainment watching movies about love, adventure or personal growth would now be a place to fear.

A trip to the concessions stands for popcorn, hot dogs, and chocolate covered raisins which satisfied their taste buds and put a smile on their lovers face might not be a good idea. Something dreadful could happen to a loved one if we left them in the car to get these items. A reminder that not all is as it seems.

A rude awakening that if it can happen in a movie theater then nothing is sacred. The police have gone, all is quiet. The lights are dim the film reels are put away. Walking to the exit the manager waves goodbye to a few employees as they drive off. He pulls his car outside the gate turns looking back at all he has built hoping his theater will survive this event. Locking the fence he makes his way to the main road to go home.

Chapter 10

REPAIR

PARAMEDICS TAKE RICHARD TO the hospital for a more in-depth inspection. Just in case there is more damage than they are able to detect. It is a busy night for the hospital since they had not seen this much action; ever. Whittier is usually a quiet place with its Eucalyptus trees blowing in the breeze and the dairy farms popping up on the side of the road. Sprinkles of orange groves covering the countryside. Definitely not a place where you would think that a serial killer would be hiding out. Or for that matter operating so efficiently that he was able to kill ten women and was working on his eleventh victim. No, this was definitely not something this little community would get over with soon.

The paramedics roll Richard into the emergency room and one of the nurses took him down to x-ray. After several different views, the x-rays are finished. Dr. Feldman came in and examined the photograph. "Well, Richard you are a very lucky man. There's a hell of a lot of bruisings and a cut on the front of your head, which we will give you some antibiotics for. The good news is that you don't have a concussion and you didn't crack your skull."

"Yeah, it's a good thing he didn't actually hit me with that hammer."

"Oh, I heard that the perpetrator was apprehended at the theater. He tried to get away, but they shot him. It says here that his name is Reynold Munday?"

"Dangerous guy and this poor girl Violet; locked up in the building behind his house. I found her, I hope she will be okay."

"Yes, Dr. Williams is attending to her right now; she is in good hands."

The nurse pushes Richard to a private room on the first floor. The doctor intended to keep him overnight just to make sure that there wasn't anything that he missed.

Richard lay in bed watching the nurses run from one room to the other. Periodically falling asleep during the night only to wake from the sounds of machines ringing informing the nurses of patients in need.

Violet is ushered into the room next to him. Tubes and monitors are attached to her body. An IV is already in place administered by the paramedics. With the help of a feeding tube, she will regain her strength back quickly. Her grandmother by her side, she finally felt safe. Awakening on and off all night to any little sound that disturbed her slumber. She would probably have that problem for a while. But she is now safe and should make a full recovery.

Reynold Munday's body is brought to the hospital. Several gunshot wounds indicated that he would not be coming out of this alive. The doctors pronounced him dead on arrival. His bloody body is rolled away on a gurney to the morgue. Weisbart and Hunter, the detectives on the case, arrive at the funeral parlor that evening to go over the body and write their findings. Next they examine the evidence taken from his home. Some of the dead bodies dated back nine years. They have their work cut out for them.

CSI continued to dig up more evidence, they are still working on the burial site. Arriving at the dairy farm Weisbart and Hunter observe the investigation. The view is too much even for the seasoned detectives. Hunter turns away throwing up his dinner; chicken alfredo. Weisbart pats his back, "Why don't you call it a night, we can get back to this tomorrow."

Nancy is given nerve pills to calm her down. The police tried to ask her several questions, but she did not have any answers for them. She also is taken to the hospital for observation. Her mother arrives to console her. She finds her in a room directly across the hall from Richard's.

Next Morning

In the morning Whittier Police Department detectives: Weisbart and Hunter arrive at the hospital to interview Richard. "Mr. Clary, how did you know that Violet was being held captive?"

"Well, I didn't know that she was in there, but Reynold kept telling me not to go anywhere near that building. You see I was working for him and I thought it was strange that he insisted I not go near that building. I think you tell somebody, not to do something there must be a reason."

"So you were working for him, and you thought something was up?" asked Weisbart, writing down all the details on a scratch pad. Only stopping to adjust his glasses.

"Yes, his behavior was strange and my curiosity got the best of me. Just so I can sleep at night I had to go check it out."

"Well, Mr. Clary, it's a good thing that you did. We found ten buried bodies behind the building and Violet would have been number eleven."

"Well, our case is almost closed we just need to speak to Violet and then we will be done. Do you think his girlfriend Nancy knew anything about it?"

"No. I don't believe so; poor thing."

The detectives walk into the next room to speak to Violet. The color has returned to her face. Her mother had taken the opportunity to clean her up; when she started feeling better. "Violet, how are you feeling?"

"Much better, Officer." Thinking, *how nice it is to be laying in a nice soft bed, clean and a full stomach.*

"I know you have been through a horrible experience. I just have to make sure that Reynold Munday is the perpetrator that hurt you?" said Officer Weisbart, he held a photo in front of her face.

Her mind starts to think back of the horrible torturing and raping he did to her.

"Yes, he's the man." She looks at his mug shot.

"Did he have any accomplices or did anyone else hurt you?"

"No sir, It was just him."

"Well, you'll be happy to hear, he is dead. He will never be hurting you again." Witnessing the fear in her eyes and then the calming effect of his words. "Now you get some rest and don't you worry about anything."

Kathy and the girls are in Richard's room visiting him. "How are you feeling honey?" Kathy gazes at him while he lays in bed.

"A lot better, the doc says that I can leave today." Still feeling an ache from his head but glad that he is on the road to recovery.

"Julia and I are going to go to see how Nancy is doing," peering at Richard for approval.

"Okay, we should be leaving within the hour." He couldn't wait to get out of the hospital; not his favorite place.

Crystal and Julia walk into Nancy's room. "Hi Nancy, we wanted to make sure you are okay," glancing around the room and then back at her. She seemed to have such a gloomy expression on her face.

"I'm as good as I can be. You know he asked me to marry him." Shaking her head in disbelief, "How could I be so wrong?"

"Don't blame yourself, there's no way you could have known," they hugged her and console her.

Standing out in the hallway the doctor scratches his signature on the release form for Richard approving his ability to leave the hospital. He must be wheeled out in a chair to the car, hospital rules they say.

Violet's condition improves and she has remained stabilized. She is released four days later. Richard and Burrell arrive at the hospital to pick her up. Rolling her out in a wheelchair to the car which Violet recognizes. Richard smiles at her placing the keys into her hands. She grins and they get into the car. Violet drives them home.

"I don't know how to repay you for giving me, my life back," she said, keeping her eyes on the road, quickly glancing at him, then back again.

"There is no need," he patted her shoulder.

Arriving home, she pulled into the driveway and parked. Stepping out she sauntered to his side of the car. Hugging him, "Thank you."

"You're welcome. Take special care of Burrell."

"I will." She opens the car door to let her out. Guiding her into the house.

Richard continues walking toward his home. "Keep the car, it really belongs to you," Richard said, waving to them as he enters his house.

Kathy has lunch ready, they stroll out on the front porch setting their meal on the table. Drinking ice tea and eating tuna fish sandwiches with potato chips, they relax. "I'm glad we made this trip," said Richard.

"Finding another serial killer is more than I bargained for," she said, standing up, stepping closer to Richard she bent and lightly kissed his forehead.

"I know, but witnessing the joyful tears on Burell's face, knowing we played a small part in that joy, well there are no words for that." He stood up and held her close to him. He has everything a man could possibly want.

"I was beside myself with fear, I almost lost you," waving her finger at his face. "In the future if you suspect wrongdoing let the police handle it."

"There was no time for that, something needed to be done right away." Raising his voice, "I will be more cautious in the future."

Crystal opens the screen door followed by Julia, they pull out their chairs to sit. Julia lifts a slice of bread off her sandwich laying potato chips on top of her tuna, smashing the slice back on top. Lifting the concoction to her mouth she sinks her teeth in and takes a healthy bite, "Mmmm."

Watching the scene Crystal said, "I guess you want to save time?"

"No, it tastes delicious this way," she took another bite.

Crystal sips her iced tea. "I think we can go home now, our mission here is finished."

Julia peered at the handsome man walking his Labrador retriever along the sidewalk. She jumped off the porch and sashayed over to the hunk. "Hi, how old is your dog?" she asked, kneeling down to pet him and rub his ears. She gazes up into the chocolate brown eyes of the muscular dog owner.

"He is five, his name is Duke," the man said, loosening his hold on the leash. He glances down her blouse through the fold as she bent over to pet the fur on the Labs back. Drawing in the beauty before him. Captivated by her grin, enticed by her fruity aroma.

Alarm bells go off in Crystal's brain like a wave of fear watching a train wreck in slow motion. Would she always feel like that? Crystal lowered herself off the porch and steps next to Julia. A wall even though imaginary is formed blocking the intruder, no further will you cross.

Julia turns toward her with a half grin, which slowly lowers. Catching the man glaring down her shirt. She stands up, "I think we should get going, bye." Mr. America continues to stroll along the walkway.

Julia grabs Crystal's hand, "I know you worry about me, but I will pay more attention and not talk to strangers."

"I'm not saying that every guy is a monster, but you do need to be more cautious with who you speak to."

"I know, the dog was so cute and the man well what a hot guy."

"Yea, he is so hot, looking down your top like an animal."

Chapter 11

STONEHENGE THE BEGINNING

RICHARD WANTED ALL THE answers; he needed to know where the book came from. If he could discover who buried the book in the ground next to Stonehenge, he could possibly be able to understand more about the history of the *Sphere.*

Once everything had settled down, they would need to leave. The happy reunion between Violet and Burrell let Richard know their journey was not in vain. Knowing that Reynold is dead and could not carry on the serial killer genetic strain left the family feeling like they have made a difference in the world. Most surprising to them all is the fact that Rex's own father was the root of his sickness. They would know the truth for sure once they got home. It was time to continue their investigation of the sphere so they would have a deeper understanding of its relevance and power.

"I'm very anxious to get home, and I'm sure you are too. But I think that we need to make one more trip at least for now," said Richard, glancing around the room reading their faces.

"Honey, where are you thinking about going?" Kathy said, putting her arms around his neck. She gazed up into his eyes.

"Well, the radiocarbon dating of the Stonehenge site indicates that the building of the monument probably began around the year 3100 BC and ends around the year 1600 BC. There seems to be a correlation between astronomical work and calendrical role in the placement of the stones. And there is evidence that Stonehenge has some type of acoustic relationship. I can't help but wonder if there's some connection between that and the sphere; since we were able to travel through time, according to sound waves from music. And Bert did say that he found a book with the drawing of the sphere in it; in that area."

"I think you might have something there," she replied, kissing him on the lips.

"Dad, I always wanted to see Stonehenge; I never got to see it."

"I can fix the sphere to the longitude and latitude near Stonehenge, but we will need to stay the distance and just observe and not get involved."

"Did you hear that Julia; we get to see Stonehenge!" Crystal claps her hands. "Yea."

"Hooray. That is so cool!" Julia shouted.

"Well, do you girls have all your gear ready?"

"Almost Dad, let me finish packing up this one bag."

"Okay honey, we're all finished," Kathy said. She picked up her luggage.

Richard huddled everyone together. He sets the sphere for 3100 BC and they all brace themselves. Everything around them begins to disappear. They can feel their bodies moving through time and space finally everything slows down. And they are standing in a meadow off in the distance and they eyewitness Stonehenge. But it's only partially built and they can observe the people who are creating it. There are about fourteen spaceships surrounding the working area. And the space capsule does not look ancient they look futuristic. Just like the one Richard found in the desert. The people are wearing the same garb too.

The workers looking very human; although they seem quite pale, are literally levitating the rocks into place. One of the workers digs a hole and starts to bury the book. Richard can hear them speaking to each other. He recognizes the language as Gaelic. One of the workers is carrying a duffel bag. He walks quite close to where they are located, but they still go undetected. There's a hole in the bottom of the duffel bag and another sphere, very much like the one that Richard has; rolls out of the bag. The worker doesn't notice that he's lost it. He travels past them, as he heads for one of the spacecraft.

Richard sees his chance and reaches out and grabs the sphere. He tucks it away in his bag. In shock and disbelief, he examines it. The sky begins to darken as evening is starting to set in. They decide to travel some distance from the workers. He hopes that when they leave to go back in their time, the workers won't notice. Finally feeling safe, Richard sets the sphere for longitude and latitude coordinates back to his home, around the date that he and Crystal had planned to go on their trip. Again the lights flash as they huddle together and everything started to fade away, finally landing in the living room of their house in Las Vegas.

"I need to call my parents and check on them, hopefully, they haven't missed me." Julia goes to the kitchen and picks up the phone and calls her parents. She carries on quite a long conversation, but everything seems to be fine she hasn't been missed. Hanging up the phone she turns to Richard, "Everything appears to be fine; maybe it worked."

Examining the bathroom window Richard cannot detect any broken glass and the back door is closed; just like he left it. He begins his search of the house and finds that everything is in order. "Well, it looks as though we are in luck everything went as planned."

Crystal goes into the living room and turns on the television set. She watches the evening news. Bonnie Brigantine is announcing the crash near the Nellis Air Force Base site. "Everything looks okay here, Dad. Bonnie is on the news about the accident site."

"The phone rings and Richard walks over and picks it up, "Hello," as he presses his finger on the counter as if it might give in.

"Hello, Richard is that you?" Bert said. He stands at a pay phone near Heathrow Airport. Checking his schedule.

"Yes, who is this?"

"It's Bert old chap, I was hoping that you got home safely."

"Ha, ha, ha, yes we did get home safely."

"Well, old boy will have a lot to talk about, we decided to come out and pay you a visit. I have so much information to share with you."

"I do too Bert, a lot more than I thought."

"We will see you on Wednesday, will you be able to pick us up at the airport?"

"Of course I will; what time?"

"Well, we are leaving Heathrow and should arrive about 6 PM at McCarran Airport."

"Great I'll see you guys then. We can catch up; love you."

"Okay, Richard we will see you chaps then, bye."

Kathy is glad to be home, the comfort of her nice cozy couch and her familiar coffee pot. She even missed her pumpkin cinnamon candle that made the house smell so inviting. She was finally home and she didn't want to leave for quite a while. A slow smile crosses her face as she lets her head fall back, "I am home."

Richard puts the duffel bags in the bar area. Then he secures the Sphere into the wall that opens up and has all of his armories. He also places the money and jewels that he has gathered on his trip inside the case. They may need these for another adventure.

Crystal turns the TV off and then turns on the stereo. *Secret agent man, secret agent man.* "Okay, that's just too funny!" Crystal and Julia start dancing around the room to the song and just having a good old time. As they sing along to the song.

Crystal and Julia giggle hysterically, "Ha, ha, ha, ha that's too funny."

"Okay, ladies, you have to know that everything that we have done is top-secret. It is going to be just between the four of us and I don't want you sharing this information with anyone; I mean nobody." As he glares at the girls.

"Don't worry Dad, we know that if this got into the wrong hands it could really be a disaster."

"Yeah, don't worry Richard; Mums the word." Julia motions her fingers crossing her heart and hoping to die.

"With this kind of power comes a lot of responsibilities. I have a very close friend named Prof. Morgan. I'm going to get a hold of him tomorrow and see about getting the two of you into the Scientific University of Virginia. That way you can be educated in the things you will need to know and use."

"You mean we might go on other adventures like this?" Crystal said.

"Knowing what we know now, I'm sure there are a few other things that we can fix," he replied.

"Well, count me in!" Julia said.

"Okay, we can talk a lot more about this tomorrow. I think I would like to get some rest. Julia, will you be staying the night?"

"Yes, it's kind of late I'll stay here."

"Good night, I'll see you girls in the morning."

Richard and Kathy head up to the bedroom. "I hope they understand how important this is."

"Honey, I'm sure they do."

Once upstairs in the privacy of their own bedroom; Kathy runs the shower. They remove their clothing and enter the cascade together. Finally, things start to feel normal. She stands at the shower head, the water washing down over her face and hair. She applies some shampoo that fills the area with the honeysuckle scent and then begins to lather her hair up. She stepped over to the side so that Richard could soak himself down. The smell is intoxicating. She applies some shampoo to Richard's hair and begins to lather him up. They get so involved with the smooth, soft suds that, they sensually rub each other down all over their bodies. She strokes her hands over his arms and up his back. He turns toward her and applies the suds to her ample bosom. Her skin begins to flush and her lips part as he held her close and kisses her, as the water rushed down over their bodies. A slow smile builds up in them. They rinse and dry each other off. And make their way to the bed.

Richard became aware of the steady beating of his own heart. The sensation of being flooded with warmth; overcomes him. He pulls her into his arms and lightly kisses her lips and then works his way down, making sure not to ignore either nipple.

Kathy shivered with pleasure as she thrust her chest to meet his lips. Her hands clenching briefly and then releasing as she slid them down his arms. Her back arched up towards him and she wrapped her hands around his head; holding him to her bosom.

She could feel his manhood pulsating between her legs and she trembled with desire. She became giddy and lightheaded. He worked his way down to the soft, moist center of her womanhood burying his face there lightly bringing her to ecstasy. She rolls over and climbs on top of him. With firm eye contact, she guided him deep inside of her. The shivers of pleasure ran over her body and tingled. Once their eyes lock, they smile in rhythm until they both explode in delight. Now, laying in each other's arms; they fall fast asleep.

Richard wakes up to use the bathroom. He turned on the light and glanced into the mirror. He takes a double-take, "What the hell?" The scar on his forehead is gone. He looks closer to the mirror, "I must be dreaming." He relieves himself and climbs back into bed.

The next morning Kathy removes the blanket and glides on her house slippers. She gently touches Richard on the shoulder to wake him up. He turns to face her and she stares at his forehead.

"Richard your cut is gone."

"What."

Richard steps out of bed and heads for the bathroom mirror, "I thought it was a dream."

"How can that happen?" Kathy said, standing next to him. She leans in to get a closer look.

"It must have something to do with the time travel," glaring at the spot where the cut was located. "Hey wait a minute, I don't have my hearing aids on and I can hear everything you said."

"If this is a side effect count me in," she wrapped the robe around her and secured the tie.

Chapter 12

SUNSHINE RESTAURANT

"THIS IS AN EXCELLENT idea, I'm famished," said Kathy. She was happy to have her appetite back.

"We can seat you right away, how is the table over by the window?" motioned the waitress with her menu.

"That will be okay," replied Richard, smiling at Kathy because he knew she is eager to eat and she was going to be fine.

The light shining through the windows illuminates the room as it bounces off of the yellow walls. Ceramic roosters of orange, tan and brown strategically placed livened up the atmosphere; giving it a warm feeling. Light, soft, piano music played in the background. The smell of bacon and pancakes fills the air signaling that it is morning. The breakfast crowd shuffles into the room filling out the majority of the restaurant, but there was one table left.

"Sunshine restaurant is cheerful," said Crystal.

"The food smells good; they have my vote," said Julia.

"We will have some orange juice and some coffee with our breakfast," said Richard.

In the center of the room, Bonnie Brigantine and her sister Diana are eating their meal. "Gosh, Bonnie do you have to hog all of the pancakes?" She sighs with exaggeration.

Bonnie lifts her fork and digs into the pancakes on Diana's plate, "I don't understand why you make such a big deal about this you are not going eat them."

"Well, I would like to decide whether I'm going to eat them or not!" She shifts back and forth in her seat.

"Dad, it looks as though things are back to normal for Bonnie," she pointed to the table in the center of the room and slightly giggles. "Ha, ha, ha."

Richard gazes over at their table and the corners of his mouth lift up. He is pleased to have stepped out from his usual routine and has daringly done the impossible. And to his amazement it has been a success. Now, he would have to find a secluded house with some acreage so he could continue his experiments with time travel and go undetected.

"Kathy, your grandma, and grandpa Tag will be coming in tonight on a plane for a visit," he said, tilting his head as he studied her with his eyes.

"Really," she whispers covering her face with her menu.

"Yes, they have some useful information for us."

The waitress returns to the table and brings their drinks, "Are you ready to order yet?"

"I will have the sausage muffin," Crystal said.

"Me too," said Kathy.

"I will have pancakes and sausage," said Julia.

"The vegetable omelet looks good, I'll have that," said Richard.

"I will be back as soon as I can with your order," she said. The waitress walks away with the menus.

"I think we should buy the Lexicon estate. It has ten acres, and it's secluded. I think it would be perfect for us."

"Dad, why would we need something so big?"

"We need something secluded and spacious just in case we need to build modules or who knows what."

The waitress returns with their breakfast. And they all become silent until she walks away. "You know Dad it's not the four of us it's actually the six of us."

"Yes, I just realized that." He continued to eat his omelet with vigor.

"What are you talking about?" Kathy asked.

"It's not just the four of us that know about the *Sphere*, your grandparents also know."

"Oh," replied Kathy. She had not seen her grandparents for many years and was excited to know they would be together this evening. She was well aware of their age and hoped they traveled safely.

Richard knew that the Lexicon estate had been on the market for over a year now. He had done a walk-through about six months ago. It had everything a person could want from a home in the country. The best feature is the ten acres of land. The house was devoid of neighbors. Slightly out of his price range but he could make use of the jewelry he gained from their trip. "Let's look at the Lexicon home again today," said Richard.

"I will call them today and set up an appointment when we get home," said Kathy. Pulling a pad and pencil out of her purse, she writes herself a note so she would not forget.

"Could I get some more coffee; please?" Richard said, staring at his empty cup.

"Here you go, sir," said the waitress as she shuffled over to the table. She filled his cup and made her rounds.

When they had finished breakfast, they left a big tip for the waitress and exit.

On the way back home Crystal said, "Did you notice that the colors on the billboards seem brighter since we traveled through time?"

"I thought it was just me, but they do look more brilliant," replied Julia, glancing at the billboards as they drove.

Richard peeped up at the signs. "I thought the same thing, it is as though having one less serial killer in the world has changed the color hue, causing a much brighter pigment."

"Actually that would be two fewer monsters in the world," Crystal said.

Kathy glimpsed at everyone in the van and said, "I kept thinking the plant life seems greener also."

"Could that happen, Richard?" Kathy's expression is amazement.

"Well, anything is possible honey," looking into Kathy's eyes, he began to think with a literal mind. "It is like a mathematical symbol or sign representing the change, like the people and the earth are expressing the positive outlook."

"Wow, I could get used to this," said Julia, the corners of her mouth curled up which caused her face to light up.

When they return to the house, Julia and Crystal decided to play cards. Kathy made a phone call to set up an appointment for 12:00 P.M. to look at the house again.

Richard checked his finances. His time travel experience has caused him to gain a substantial amount of extra cash.

They drove to the Lexicon house taking the Highway 160. It only took them twenty minutes. The weather was still cold, but Vegas never felt that chilly. The road was clear and empty; except for a few burros and a rabbit here and there.

Making a right after the Mini Mart they continued to drive up and through the mountain. Once they reached the top, a herd of wild Mustang gathered near the rod-iron gate; the entrance to the estate. Miss Baron, the real estate agent, swooshed her foot back and forth on the ground in front of her as she fed the horse a handful of grain. "Hello," she said, waving them down. "It is a pleasure to see you again."

Richard pulled forward, smiling. "How are you?"

"Great, I have extraordinary news, the price has dropped by twenty-thousand," reaching her hands up in the air with glee.

Parking the vehicle at the gate, Richard stepped out of the car. He raised his hand and patted the Mustang on her mane. Slowly the herd moved on as the three other doors flew open and Kathy, Julia, and Crystal exited.

Miss Baron walked them through the entrance of the property and began the grand tour. She would make a pretty penny on the property if she could only get the sale. "If you remember the estate is on ten acres and has a well with the water rights. You have one acre just of fruit trees. A lavish pool with an adjoining spa. And, of course, a horse stable set up for eight horses. It is zoned for boarding if you so choose."

"You said, they lowered the price twenty-thousand?" As he rubbed his chin and pinched it.

"Yes, everything is the same but the price. I was looking over our last paperwork from six months ago. Holding a file in her hand she opens it and checks her figures once more. That was the only hold up last time." Reaching the front door, she unlocked the entrance, "I will wait by the pool so you can talk and do your walk through." She walked along the cobblestone walkway around the house heading to the backyard where the pool is located.

"Honey, can you believe our luck!" shouted Kathy, as she did a jig, clinching her teeth, trying not to look too overjoyed.

Gazing out the front door he could spy the girls out by the horse stable. "You don't look like the only one who is happy."

Crystal is measuring the footage of the stable. The corners of her mouth jet up when she turns toward her father's direction and sees her mother's excitement. She waves, "It looks like a done deal, Julia."

"How awesome," she replied, walking through the stables admiring the woodwork.

Kathy steps inside and heads for the kitchen. The soft sound of her pitter-patter walk, across the stone tile, allowed the listener to feel the emptiness of the room as the echo drifted through the house. She is impressed with the orange, brown, and black speckled marble counter tops. The pale sherbert painted walls added an inviting warmth to the kitchen. "I feel like, I am home," she gushed. "The medium brown cupboards are perfect."

"I like the six- foot block wall that encloses the whole property," Richard replied, gazing out the kitchen window. "It is a perfect fortress for safety, considering our new job; vocation."

Crystal and Julia enter the house and promptly climb the stairs to the second floor. Since the master bedroom is located on the first floor,

Crystal would have her choice of four bedrooms. She knew the second floor, the master bedroom would be her selection if that met with the approval of her mom and dad.

"What a splendid view you will have from your bedroom window," Julia remarked, overlooking the orchard.

"Can you believe this?" pointing at the horse stable.

"Yes, I can and you deserve every good thing that life has to offer," she replied. "Saving my life and your mother's is the greatest act of selflessness I have ever experienced."

Crystal walked over to the window and stood next to her best friend. She put her arm on her shoulder and pulled her in, "You, my friend are worth more than a hundred friends."

"I am indebted to both you and your father," she smiled. "Whatever your dad has planned I am in it for the long haul."

"You do not owe us anything, I am just glad to have you alive and well."

"I know that, but I want to make a difference in the world just like you."

"You do create a divergence. Every day you were gone, I felt lost, now I feel stronger."

"That is what friends are for, we make each other better people."

They walked down the staircase into the kitchen and waited for Richard to say something.

Richard walks through the double doors out to the pool. Standing in front of Miss Baron, he said, "We will take it. Draw up the papers."

"Yes Mr. Clary," she replied. "I will do that tonight. You can sign tomorrow."

In the morning, Richard met Miss Baron in her office. He signs the papers and she moved closer to him viewing the paperwork over his shoulder.

"You will be able to close and can move in by the end of the month."

"Great," he said standing up he handed the contract to her.

She rests her hand on him, smiling, "What are you doing later?" Moving closer to his face. "We could meet at my place for a drink."

"Miss Baron, I am a happily married man and today is our anniversary," staring her down.

"Oh, please don't get upset with me. I am sorry," backing away from his side.

"Good day Miss Baron," he said walking out of the office shaking his head. He thought her attractive even a raving beauty but could not understand her forwardness toward a married man. He has the best wife that life has to offer, waiting for him at home. They have built a loving house together, not with stone or mortar but the kind of home that is not made of such things. Their abode is each other.

Chapter 13

WARPED

WEDNESDAY EVENING CAME QUICKLY. Richard arrived at McCarran Airport around 6:00 P.M. He waited patiently in the luggage claim area. He spotted his in-laws, as they gathered their bags at carousel number twenty-two. They had aged quite a bit and he expected that, but it still made him sad. He knew they had to be at least in their eighty's. And here they were helping him. Kathy's family was unfaltering, but they completely exceeded his expectations.

"I see your plane arrived on time," he gave them each a warm embrace and then gathers up their luggage. To his surprise, the bags were hefty.

"Yes, we managed to beat the storm that was headed into Heathrow by one hour," said Bert. "Otherwise we would have been delayed by five hours or more."

"I managed to get a parking garage closest to the carousel. So we only have a short distance to go," he said lifting one eyebrow as he smiled hoping that would bring some comfort to the weary travelers.

"Splendid, I am quite tired from our travels." Elizabeth clenched her coat tightly around her as a cold breeze hit them when the door opened to a walkway directed towards the garage.

Once they had deposited their luggage inside of the van, they were able to sit down and relax. Richard turned the heater on to ward off the cold weather. They were finally situated in a more private atmosphere and could now speak openly.

"Richard, I was able to extract more information about the *Sphere* by doing some research at the Royal Army Library. I was able to find many books on the subject. Some underground books I discovered in an old bookstore."

"Is that why your luggage is so hefty?" Richard said, gazing at the luggage behind him.

"I was not allowed to check out the books from the Royal Army Library, but the underground books that I discovered at that old bookstore; I brought them along."

Driving out of the parking garage, Richard wondered if any of the people that Bert worked with noticed his interest in the subject.

He gazed at Bert and asked, "Do you think any of your colleagues are aware of your interest?"

Scratching his chin, Bert replied, "I don't believe so, nobody seemed interested and I kept a watchful eye, making sure I wasn't being followed."

Richard plans to add the books to his archive. Anything related to *time travel* or the *Sphere* would be cataloged and stored for future reference. The wheels were spinning in his mind. He glances a headlight pulling out behind him. Continuing to view the car from his rearview mirror. He made a left onto the freeway. From a three-car distance, he could still see the vehicle trailing behind them. "Don't look now but I have spotted a car following us, I think we can lose him at the underpass."

"Who could it be?" Bert questioned. "No one is aware of our travels," he arched his eyebrows with a bewildered expression on his face.

Richard made a hard right just in time to become invisible from the traffic, allowing no time for the driver to make the turn. "I think we lost him."

"What kind of vehicle was it?" Bert inquired, rubbing his forehead as though he had a headache.

"A white Sedan, but I think it was a rental car," Richard continued to stare through the mirror.

"I will drive around for a bit just in case. I would not want to lead them to our house," he said navigating around for about fifteen minutes. Not noticing anyone trailing behind him, he headed for the house.

Richard carries their bags into the foyer, "Honey, your grandparents are here."

Kathy stepped out of the kitchen holding a hand cloth while drying a plate. She sat the dish and towel down. She embraced her Nana Elizabeth, "How was your trip, Nana?"

"I love to travel my dear, but the body has other plans," holding her so dearly. Shaking her head at herself for feeling exhausted.

Bert joined the group hug, "I must say I'm not as chipper these days, but it is lovely to see you, Lass."

"Richard told me all about their trip to London, seems they had quite an adventure." She led them to the dining table and stepped into the kitchen to make them a spot of tea. Returning to the table with a china pot with their favorite PG Tips tea and chocolate cake. Pouring them each a cup and slicing the cake laying a piece on each plate. She pulls out her seat and sits down.

"Yes, imagine my shock when Richard explained the whole ordeal to me." Bert lifted his cup to sip and placed it back down, "I found some interesting reading material. We thought it was folklore but in light of our discovery it is quite the contrary."

Bert stands up and walks to the suitcase, unzipping the baggage, he pulls out a book. He hobbled back over to the table and lifts the novel. "See this here book is really an ancient manuscript," he hands it to Kathy.

Richard peers over her shoulder to get a gander of the new found artifact. Discerning visibly the pages; searching for the insight. "Yes, this will be a significant addition to the collection."

"You would not believe what Crystal and I were able to do because of the sphere," Richard said. "We went to the future. We actually found a cure for cancer."

"Really Richard, that is marvelous!" Bert said.

"Yes, and they gave it to me," she looked at her hands and feet. The curve of her mouth said everything.

"I knew something had happened because everything seemed more illuminate," said Elizabeth.

"The problem is that you may have been followed," Richard said. "If that is the case you could be in danger," studying their reaction.

"We are old my dears, nothing to worry about; we will be okay," said Bert.

"I think you should stay here, in the U.S. I just bought a ten- acre estate. We will have plenty of rooms. I could use your help with the research."

"Of course I will help," he said slapping his knee.

"We will be able to correct some of the problems of our world." He sat back down at the table and patted Bert on the shoulder, "Thank you so much for all your help."

Bert grinned and rested his hand on Richard's, "Maybe we could do something about the hole in the ozone layer."

"Fantastic Idea!"

They spent the rest of the evening analyzing the books Bert discovered. Lengthy discussions about theories filled the room until they broke out a chalkboard and wrote the formulas out.

The woman grew tired and went off to bed, but the men stayed up until the wee hours of the morning. Finally exhausted they too slept.

Chapter 14

THE RESEARCH LAB

OVER THE NEXT NINE months, Richard and his family move in and organize the Lexicon Estate. Bert and Richard gather equipment for the research lab. Meticulously Richard put his library together, all of his books alphabetized and cataloged. One section contains everything that is government related to (UFO's) Unidentified Flying Objects. The second section holds everything that is associated with the Sphere: books, drawings, and old folklore that was discovered in England. The third section contains all data he has obtained in Nevada. The last section is dedicated to all of his time travel experiences. He documents each involvement by the date, time, and place. He also pinpoints the coordinates of each location.

Richard decides to build a module which he plans to use when they transfigure. The men keep themselves busy measuring the size of the module along with the latitude and longitude of its location.

Crystal and Julia go to the library and collect anything remotely related to time travel. Each night they read the collection of books, filling their minds with the concepts. Richard and Bert go over the information; sharing the theory on the chalkboard.

Kathy and Elizabeth arrange the furniture and unpack the boxes. Hanging curtains and making the meals. Everyone has adapted to their new way of life.

Not wanting to see her grandparents struggle up and down the stairs of the house they decided to give them the bedroom downstairs. Richard and Kathy would take the bedroom upstairs. Crystal would be down the hall from them. The study is next to the downstairs bedroom.

Walking into Richard's study one morning Crystal said, "Dad I'm ready to purchase the Lipizzaner Stallion," she smiles as she glances over the sale section of the newspaper.

Looking up from the book he is reading, he studies her face, "Do you feel that you have found the right stallion for the breeding stable?"

Pointing at the middle section of the paper she lays it down on the desk, "Yes, Father this is the perfect stallion."

Richard studied the article paying close attention to the cost. "I know you're anxious to get started, but I wonder if this is a fair price."

"I've done my homework, Dad, this is a reasonable price. If he's in good condition, but we'll have to go look at him today because if he is in a decent state, this deal won't last long."

"Okay, let's go today I can leave in about an hour is that soon enough?" He closed his book and stood up lifting his hand up to rub his chin.

Crystal picks up the newspaper turns and heads for the door, "I'll be ready."

She purposely saved up her money for this very moment. Now she could visualize her dreams coming true. Breeding horses can be profitable and time efficient. Lipizzaner is great for training, breeding and overall splendid horses.

The Lipizzaner Ranch is located in Amargosa Valley. The drive is relatively short from their current location. About twenty miles pass Pahrump. Crystal already hitched up the horse trailer, quite confident they would be of high breeding. She has eyed the ranch for two years now and found them to be beyond blemish.

Richard knew his daughter to be a good judge especially when it came to matters involving the equine business. He could count on her to research the field until she is completely satisfied with her selection.

The ranch is impressive pulling up to the gate. The spread is five-hundred acres. Half of the farm is, of course, alfalfa fields.

The attendant opens the entrance. "You can park over to the left," he pointed to an open parking spot.

Richard parks the van. They step out of the vehicle and are guided to the office. Inside the wall is covered with photos of the horse lineage of their top breeder. The ancestry dated back one-hundred years. Apparently a family business since the gentleman sitting at the desk could not be older than Crystal. He smiled in her direction.

"Good afternoon, you must be Miss Clary," he reached out to shake her hand.

"Yes, and you are Mr. Ackerman," shaking his hand. "This is my father, Mr. Clary."

"How nice to make your acquittance," they shake hands and walk toward the stables.

"Shylow is groomed and ready for inspection," he opens the gate and escorts Crystal inside.

She walks over to the stud. Inspecting his teeth, nose, and ears. Then lifting his hoof and cleaning out the debris. He rubs his nose on her sleeve. She pats him on the neck.

"May I ride him around the pen?"

"Sure, let me get his halter."

He returns and places the bit in Shylows mouth. No signs of an argument from the Lipizzaner. Crystal jumps up on his back and heads for the corral. The stallion is smooth and handles like a champ. She walks him around the perimeter. He whinnies to a brood mare. She whinnies back.

"That would be Ginger," he said, as he steers Shylow over to the other horse and rubs his hand along her mane. A few more discussions between the horses ensues. Crystal dismounts and ties the strap to the hitch. She came alongside the man viewing the other horse.

"I can throw her in for an extra five-hundred." He watched for an expression, "You would be doing me a favor since they have been together for so long."

"Is she good breeding?"

"Yes, she has a couple of good years left in her."

"It's a deal," she said shaking his hand.

"By the way my first name is Chuck."

"Mine is Crystal."

"I will get their papers ready, and meet you back at the office." He ambles back to the administrative center.

"It seems you have acquired two great looking champions instead of one," Richard said, with his shoulders back and a gleam in his eye.

"I can start breeding right away," she said, scarcely able to contain herself.

Crystal loaded the stallion and the mare into the trailer. Locking the gate, she returns to the office. She paid the man and obtains a receipt along with the papers. Making sure they are not related by lineage.

"I will take care of them while you are taking the fall semester," said Richard.

"Thanks, Dad."

On the way home a storm hovers above, pelting rain dashes down and the wind rocks the trailer. Part of the road is washed out which made them move slowly through the canyon. Richard is not used to hauling a trailer but navigates in spite of his impairment. A herd of Mustang trample across the pool of water, running spiritly as though they have a mysterious secret place to go.

Crystal watched them run out of sight. Now viewing the road up ahead she said, "Stop! There is a large branch in the way."

Richard halts the vehicle. Crystal ran into the street and moves the log to the edge of the highway. She races back, soaking wet, examines the horses and hops into the van.

Five more miles and they will be home. Richard felt foolish for not checking the weather report. He finally reaches their turn off. Making a left they edge through the mountain. Water has subsided on the road. They are home.

"That was crazy," she said, exiting the vehicle she removes the gate and lets the horses down, one by one, she escorts them to their corral. Richard unloads the bales of hay which had smartened the deal.

Chapter 15

COLLEGE-BOUND

"I REALLY LOVE THIS plan: get a college education in Quantum Reality 501, Archaeology 101, and Physics 201," Crystal said, sliding her finger along the edge of the curtain.

"I still can't get over the fact that we get to share our dorm room together," replied Julia, folding her blouse and resting it in the second drawer.

"If you don't mind I'll take the bed by the window." To her surprise, she smiled.

"That's okay Crystal, you can have the bed by the window, and I will take the one closer to the bathroom."

Peering out the window of the third story, Crystal gazed down at the open marble square, with all of the students walking back and forth preparing their dorm rooms for the fall season. The air has already started to turn cool, as the oak leaves, fall from the trees very lightly and float across the open square. Colors of red, orange and yellow covered the ground. Crystal can see her father, approaching with another box in his hands. He makes his way up the stairs until he reaches their dorm room.

Opening the door, he entered and sat the box on the bed. "Now I want you to listen carefully to Professor Morgan, he's a good friend of mine and he will give you the individual attention that you will need for this project."

Spinning around he headed for the door, securely locking it.

"What do you have in the box, Dad?"

"I consider it survival gear, I'm trusting you to only use this in case of an emergency. Otherwise, I want you to keep it safely locked up in this safe," he pointed to the obnoxious metal object inside the closet.

"We will," Crystal replied, picking up the sphere and loading it into the safe. Twisting the headlock. "Secure."

They escort Richard back down to his car gave him hugs and kisses and said their goodbyes, waving to him as he drove off in the van.

Driving out the entrance to the University. He stopped took one look at the Marquis, *Scientific University of Virginia, founded in 1809.* Then he continued to push on; heading home.

They sashay back to the dorm, noticing that everyone is wearing the maroon and green colors, which represented their college. Once they reached the entrance of their dorm room, a young woman stepped out of her room which was directly next-door. She turned and smiled at them her dark brown eyes sparkled as she flips her brown hair out of her face.

"Hi, my name is Jewel, I have the dorm, next-door."

Gazing at her, they could not help but notice the *emerald brooch* on her blouse. *Could she possibly be, no it could not be, they thought.*

"Hi, my name is Crystal and this is my best friend, Julia. We are from Las Vegas," trying not to stare and the sparkling brooch.

"I'm from Whittier, California," she said, pulling her Cashmere sweater over her shoulders.

They looked her up and down. Turned toward each other shrugged their shoulders and took turns shaking hands. "How would you like to join us for lunch?" asked Julia.

Feeling a sense of relief she shook her head and said, "Yea that would be great!"

Walking to the local Pizza Palace, Crystal thought about the shift of change caused by their *time travel*. How many changes had occurred because of their experience? Would they be good, positive changes or would their meddling; have an adverse effect? Only time would tell. So far, *nothing* negative happened.

The knowledge that Reynold was the one with the Serial Killer genetic marker, not Nancy gave a glimmer of hope to Crystal. "So... is your mother here with you?" Crystal said.

"No, she left yesterday," Jewel replied. "She and Dad had to get back to their jobs," she smiled.

"What kind of work do they do?" asked Julia, her arms swinging from side to side as she strolled along the sidewalk seeming to not have a care in the world.

"My dad is a clothing store owner. He met my mom when she applied for a job at his clothing store. They fell in love and the rest is history."

She had the same bounce in her step that Crystal noticed in her mother. "What is your mom's name?"

Why so interested in my parents, she thought. "Nancy, her name is Nancy Gottschalk."

Arriving at the restaurant, Crystal opened the door and they filed in. Finding a free table they seated themselves near the window at the far left.

"What do your Parents do?" Jewel asked, fidgeting with the paper napkin, in an uneasy manner.

"Well, my dad works for the government."

"My dad has a carpet cleaning company," Julia smiled.

The waitress brought them a menu and glasses of water. "Would you like to start with a drink?" she asked. "We have Coke, 7up or root beer."

Looking the list over Crystal said, "How about a root beer and I think I would like pepperoni pizza."

"Do you want to split a large pizza?" Julia asked.

"Yes, but I would like a coke with mine," replied Jewel.

"Okay, and I would also like coke."

"Great a large pepperoni pizza and our drinks, thanks."

"I will be right back." The waitress went on her way to the kitchen.

Crystal walked over to the pool table, pulled some coins out of her pocket and deposited them into the slots, "Who wants to play first?"

"I do," Jewel walked over to the pool sticks scratching her chin as she made her selection. Chalking her stick she was ready.

Crystal sashayed over to the opposite side of the table and racked the balls, "I rack you break."

Jewel grabbed the white ball lining it up from the left side. Crystal removed the frame and stepped back, hanging the object back on the wall. With a crack, the balls went flying across the table; dispersing. Still none entered a pocket.

"Your turn."

Crystal measured the situation and said, "One in the side pocket." She lowered her cue and lined up the angle. Snap; and the ball went in.

"I better watch out you're pretty good."

"Five in the corner pocket," reaching over with a backhand move she lightly hit the ball and it rolled into the corner pocket.

"Hey, she is a hustler, did you see that backhand?" resting her hand on one hip.

"She is pretty good," replied Julia, peering from the table.

"Three in the side pocket," Crystal lightly tapped the ball and it sunk in the pocket.

"I think I'll just sit down, let me know if it's my turn." With her shoulders hanging flat, she sat back down in the booth.

The waitress brought their drinks to the table. "Thank you," said Julia.

She cleaned a few tables and headed back to the kitchen.

In the far right corner of the pizzeria, a man with a black hoodie slumped over his meal eating in silence. He peered over occasionally.

"It's your turn," Crystal slid into the booth, taking a sip of her drink.

"Finally!" Lifting herself, she walked to the table and sized up her options. Pointing her cue in several directions until she found the magic angle. "Fifteen in the side pocket," pop, and in it went, "Hooray."

"Ten in the corner pocket," reaching across as far as she could. Crack. "Darn."

"Okay, the pro you're up," laying her stick against the booth.

Crystal sprung into action. Chalking her stick, approaching the table with a vengeance, hoping to wrap this up before the pizza arrived. "Four in the corner pocket." Snap! "Two in the side pocket." Crack! "Six in the corner pocket hitting off the seven with them both will falling in." Crack-crack!

Finally, only the eight ball left. The guy in the hoodie could only try not to watch. Glaring from the corner of his eye. *Competitive isn't she*, he thought.

"The eight ball in the side pocket." Tap. "Woo-hoo."

"What did she beat her own score?" Jewel asked, rolling her eyes.

"Don't take it so personal, she is just exceptional." Sipping her drink, "She has a lot of excellent qualities; subtlety is not one of them.

Sitting back down at the table she sipped her root beer, smiling. She really never understood why winning a pool game felt so good but; it did.

Pizza arrived, the aroma rising to meet their noses. Each reaching for a slice to fill their plate.

"Mmmm… so good, what a reward," she said taking a bite. A little sauce smudged on her cheek. She dabbed her face with a napkin.

"Thanks for inviting me to lunch," Jewel said, devouring her slice.

"I like your outfit, is it from your dad's store? Julia asked, touching the shoulder of her sweater.

"Yea, my mom has excellent taste. She usually does all the ordering for the shop."

"It is so soft, is that Cashmere?" Juila asked.

"Yes, I'm so glad I don't have an allergy to the fur." Taking her hand and rubbing her forearm, "If you need anything just let me know, my mom can get it at cost."

"That is so sweet of you," Crystal said.

"Let's go to the Klondike Mall and get some curtains for our room," Julia said, finishing her last bite.

"Okay," Crystal wiped her face with the napkin and stood up.

They shuffled out the door single file until they reached the sidewalk. Unknown to them, they were being followed from a distance. The guy with the black hoodie kept an eye on them as they strolled through the park; a shortcut to the mall.

"I think we will have a fun semester," Crystal said. "The archeology class will be interesting."

"Oh, I'm taking that class too," Jewel replied. "I think the study of humans could reveal some surprises."

"I especially hope I don't miss the part about grabbing the cavewoman's hair and dragging her back to the cave...Ha, Ha, Ha," Crystal laughed so hard her stomach hurt.

Jewel laughed, "Ha, Ha." *And then — a far-reaching look occupied her face.*

"Are you okay, Jewel?" Julia asked.

"I'm sorry, my mom told me a story about how she almost married a *Serial Killer*, and the thought of a woman being dragged brought that to mind."

"Really, is she okay?" Julia stepping in front of her, staring into her eyes.

"Yes, they caught him before he could hurt her."

"I am so sorry she experienced that," said Crystal. She took her hand and lightly patted it with the other. "Sometimes bad things happen to good people."

They walked in the front door of the mall entrance, seeing the arcade on the right.

To take her mind off the sad ordeal that her mother suffered, they decided to play video games in the Galaxy Arcade. Rock music blared from the room. Lights set on low brought more attention to the lit up game boards. Crystal climbed into the space invader cubby in the hopes of beating her highest score.

Julia put a coin in the air hockey game. Jewel sashayed to the other end of the table grabbing the blocker; prepared for action.

Air flowed across the table lightly floating the disc. Julia gave it a shove landing just short of the pocket. Jewel lunged forward shooting it straight into the pocket.

"Woo-hoo."

"I can see this is your game," said Julia. Noticing the spark returning to her eyes.

They played back and forth until exhaustion. Jewel whipped Julia's butt.

Crystal noticed the same guy from the pizza joint sitting on a bench across from the game room. She took note of his presence; then let it go.

She tapped Julia on the shoulder. "We should find some curtains in the Broadway," said Crystal.

"Okay." She put her blocker down. "Let's go."

They strolled toward the Broadway department store. One lady was screaming at her child, "No, you cannot have any more candy." The little girl has tears running down her face. The woman dabs her tongue on a napkin wiping the chocolate off her cheek.

A pregnant woman and her husband look intently at a baby crib from the furniture store window.

Reaching the store they walked up to the first counter. "Do you know where the curtains are located?" Crystal asked, opening her purse and popping a tic-tac in her mouth.

"Sure, the second floor, make a right."

Riding the escalator to the second floor, Crystal catches a glimpse of the black hoodie from the mirrored walls. Shaking her head. She thought *I must be getting paranoid.*

"Did you hear about the dance tomorrow night?" Julia raised her hands above her head, swaying her hips.

"No, there is a dance," replied Julia.

"The curtains should be next to the comforters, over there," said Crystal, standing on her tiptoes to view the section.

"Oh Crystal, look. Red roses." Julia pulled the package off the shelf.

"Perfect, red roses," she replied. Admiring the colors.

"Hey, they have matching comforters to," said Crystal.

They each grabbed a quilt and walked to the check-out stand. The clerk rang up their orders, bagged the items and said her goodbyes. They— then headed back to the dorm.

"We'll I for one would love to go to the dance tomorrow night. Shall we make a night of it girls?" Crystal's mouth curved up at the ends.

"Great I'll see you then." Jewel opened her door and waved goodbye.

Crystal and Julia carried their comforters inside and placed them on the bed.

She peeked out her window and Crystal could see the guy in the black hoodie again. She thought to herself, *he must go to our college, I'm over thinking this.*

Chapter 16

FOLLOWED

"I'M GOING TO THE library, I will be back soon," Crystal said. She walked out of the dorm to get an early start on a few books she hopes the library with its extensive collection will carry. She walks on the trail through the campus on the far side of the park; she could hear the birds chirp, nestled in warm nests high in the trees. Many people were heading out to church. Sunday mornings are always peaceful. Chilly morning air sent a shiver up her back. She passes a row of bushes with Poplar trees planted between each individual shrub. From the corner of her eye, she saw the black hoodie in the distance. Fear gripped her mass. At first she was stunned, then her mind overrides her body. She creeps into the bushes, lowering her head. Prickly hairs on her neck stood straight out, like a cat when it is frightened.

Crystal could see him as he passes the row of bushes. He has the hoodie hanging down over his head, which made it difficult to view his face, but she could tell he had a medium build body. She reaches into her purse pulling out a small can of hairspray, lightly shaking the bottle until it felt sufficient.

Stepping out of the bushes, quietly following behind the man, she crept until he turned to face her. Without warning, she presses down on the nozzle, spraying him directly into the eyes.

"Ah…What…Hell!" He screams and falls down to his knees, as he rolls in pain.

"Tom— is that you?"

"Crystal why did you do that," he said wiping his eyes as tears rush forward like a river.

"Me, why are you following me, moreover how did you get here?" standing over him ready to pounce with her purse gripped like a weapon.

He finally could see after several minutes. Staying on the ground he looked up at her. "I am not here to hurt you," fixing his gaze on her. "I am wondering why you are here?"

He could not be here unless he can travel in time, she thought, lowering her purse, she sat down next to him. Picking at blades of grass, she tossed them, "Okay, you must be able to travel through time. Otherwise, this would not make sense."

"Okay, you got me," removing his hoodie he wipes his face. Setting it down on the ground next to him. "I am a time traveler, have been all my life. What I'm about to tell you, cannot be repeated."

"Okay," she said, scooting closer to listen to the story.

"I came to the planet you call Earth; we call it *Talamh*. I arrived 3100 BC. My job was to build the Stonehenge. It is like a way station spot so we can hop from our planet to your planet along with our time travel object: the Sphere. If the stones are placed correctly, it sensitizes the sound wave. Something went wrong; I tried to take off for home but could not lift off."

"Where is your ship, now?"

"I have a cloaking device, It has shielded the craft for a very long time. Over the years, I replaced the crystal which keeps the buffer working."

"You have any other people with you?"

"No, I have been all alone until I saw you. When I met you in the pub back in London, that is when I discovered, I am not alone."

"How do you mean?"

"Crystal I first met you in the future; Professor Morgan's class. So when I saw you again in the past; I knew."

"So you came back here again to make sure?" Holding her hands up and out.

"Yes, I had to make sure—you are for real."

"I am for real," she said, as she looked him up and down.

"But once I got here I became nervous." He looked down at the ground, "I have never revealed myself to anyone." He gazed at the grass, "I know you can only move through time with the object, and then I realized somehow you must have the other Sphere."

"Okay, I believe you. But we will have to tell my dad he is the only one who could help you."

"I don't want to become something the military wishes to study."

"Don't worry that will not happen." She smiles, "My Dad will not let that happen."

"I'm trusting you," he said. "The spaceship will only leave this planet if two spheres are operational."

"We can actually help each other," she relayed.

"How?"

"You can help us understand the sphere, what the capabilities are and my dad can help you get back home."

Tinstelisa his home was once a flourishing planet before the sun began to burn out. Many of her inhabitant's moved on to Alcatisa the world with three moons and one sun. Since she could support life, he wondered if his mother and father made it safely there or had they moved on to another ecosphere? He had to find out.

"Okay, I am willing to talk to your father," he stood up and reached his hand out to lift her from the ground. "But I will not be poked and probed like a pin cushion," he said, wiping the grass from his behind.

"I'm sorry about the hairspray." She picked up the garment and handed it over to him.

"How did you learn that trick?" he asked, pulling the hoodie back over his head.

She stood in front of him relaying her adventure and the classes she took when her best friend disappeared; Self-defense education.

Rambling on, she told him the whole story, even how they ended up in London.

His eyes watched her as the animation of their time travel unfolded. Surprised they have learned so much on their own. The scent of wildflowers surrounds him like an envelope. He is captivated by her alluring eyes which reached down into his soul drawing him in deeper until he was completely enchanted. He chaperoned her through the park. Hanging on her every word he realizes the feeling of freedom that accompanied his confession. Sharing his truth opened his ability to see a future. As she continues to share her story, he feels the warmth radiating throughout his body. Rejuvenated by adrenaline his heart drumming in his chest. This is the third time he has encountered her and each moment feels the same. His face beams; euphoria widens his eyes. He tries to contain his emotion not wanting to run her off. Quiverin' and looking down to hide his grin.

She felt her heartbeat like a constant fast train moving quickly to its destination with no stops along the way. She shivered but not from the cold. Holding her breath in slightly glancing away hoping he didn't notice her desire rising when they made eye contact. Her skin flushing she bit her lip in uneasiness. Could he tell what her thoughts were?

"Why don't we grab a bite to eat," he said, pointing to the taco eatery on the corner.

"Yea, I am hungry." She accompanied him down the sidewalk to the restaurant.

"The fish tacos are terrific." He opens the door to let her in.

Now inside, they situated themselves at a booth. "I can make a call to my dad at the pay phone, they have one near the restroom."

The waitress brought them a menu and some glasses of water. "Here you go. Would you like a drink?"

"Yes, I would like a Coke," he said.

"I will have the diet Coke." She picks up her napkin and places it on her lap.

The waitress returns to the busy kitchen. Her drink order in her mind.

Fish taco aroma floats through the dining room inviting the growls and gurgle sounds of the stomach and the mouth to water in anticipations. Crystal became embarrassed by the uncontrollable sounds coming from her gut. How could her body betray her this way? This was no time to bring unladylike attention to her person. She already has a hard time keeping her eyes from being mesmerized by his muscular physic. His eyes seemed to perceive deep into her thoughts which at this point wasn't something she cares to share. Why— she was attracted to him, even his voice sounds like a come – hither which she found hard to control. "How is it that you don't look ancient?"

"Oh, the thing about *time travel,* well you don't age." He smiled a happy grin.

"Really?" she said, viewing her hands.

"Yes, a side effect."

"Will that happen to me?"

"So far as I'm aware of, yes."

"My father had a cut on his head and in the morning it was gone."

"Another excellent side effect, no scars."

Anna, the waitress, returns to the table. "Here are your drinks, are you ready to order?"

"Would you like to try the fish tacos?" he asked, glancing in her direction.

"Yes, two tacos."

"We will have four tacos."

"Coming right up." She picks up the menus and returns to the kitchen.

"I think I will call my dad, I'll be back," as she strolls to the pay phone and deposits a coin. She waits while the sound of ringing continues. Finally, he picks up.

"Hello."

"Hey Dad, I need to talk to you about an important matter."

"What's up."

"You remember our trip when we met Tom, the guy from the pub?"

"The one who gave us a ride?"

"Yea."

"Well, he is here, I can't say much on the phone, but he is here."

"There, you mean at the college?"

"Yea, we are having lunch right now."

"Lunch, you talked to him."

"I am talking to him right now at the taco shop by the college."

"I will be there as soon as I can." His demeanor is serious, "Wait there."

"Everything is okay Dad, just come when you can we need to talk."

"Okay pumpkin, see you soon."

By the time, Crystal returns to the table her father walked into the eatery and said, "Are you all right?"

"I'm all right, Dad!" Happy he can move that fast, this could come in handy if they had a serious problem, she thought. "You remember Tom?"

"Hi," Tom said, "Would you like a taco too?"

"Oh, okay," he said, sliding into the booth.

Anna brought the tacos and Tom asked for two more. She went to fetch the additional food.

"Dad, it seems that Tom has been a *time traveler* from the beginning. He can't get back home. He recognized me since he saw me in the future, Professor Morgans class. When he viewed me again in the past; well he realized we must also move through time."

"This is fantastic!" Richard said. "How have you been surviving?"

"Fine."

"I don't understand, you seem to be about twenty-one."

"We were just discussing that, once you transfigure, you stop aging."

"Really?" he scratched his head. "I recall a gash on my head that just disappeared."

"Yes, it is quite surprising, isn't it?" Tom said.

Finished with dressing the tacos Anna deposits the food on the table, "Would you care for anything else?"

"No, thank you," Richard said.

She moved back to the kitchen.

"I want to make it perfectly clear that I will share my knowledge with you, but I will not become an experiment; no government involvement, agreed?"

"Don't worry about that, I may work for the government, but this will not be revealed to the officials; that would just complicate everything." He sighed. "The less they know, the safer everyone will be."

"I'm glad we agree on that matter," he said, taking a bite out of his taco.

"Why didn't you mention this to me when I met you in London?"

"I was surprised, I thought I was the only time traveler, and well—frantic." He took another bite. "You need to understand, this has not happened since I got here. I have never told a soul about it and I'm hoping I can trust you."

Crystal sips her drink, silent as the men spoke. She knew he could trust her dad. The thing about Richard that she knew all too well but evaded most was his loyalty. She hopes it is not misplaced. What did they really know about this guy? Was he telling the truth? She wanted to believe him, he seems honest, but looks can be deceiving. She thought her a good judge of character but her father is the one who has an uncanny ability to sniff out deception. Crystal would leave that decision to him.

They finished their lunch and escort Crystal back to the library. She collects the books for her studies while the men discuss in more detail about the phenomenon of the law of nature and the observable experience of their *time travel*.

Gathering all the books, they accompany her back to the dorm. Once inside her room they decide the best course of action would be for Tom to return with Richard to Lexicon Estate. They would resume their research there.

Chapter 17

RETURNING THROUGH BY WAY of the module, Richard opens the door and escorts Tom pass the horse stable up the cobblestone walkway to the front door entrance. He unlocks the entry and announces he has company. Tom enters the ingress followed by Richard.

"Hello, anyone home?" He peers around the room then walks to the kitchen, "They must have gone out."

"What an elaborate home you own," Tom said, viewing the granite countertops.

"I decided to go all out. My wife always wanted this house; the first time she laid eyes on it."

"You certainly have an abundance of space," he could hear his own echoing footsteps.

"You see I lost her, she passed away from cancer. When I realized, I could travel through time and redeem her life back, at that moment I concluded she would receive all the comforts that I may possibly offer." He opened the refrigerator and lifts two sodas out, handing one to him.

Tom twists the top off and takes a swig. Walking around the kitchen and then plod to the living room. Richard follows him. They sit down on the couch.

"So tell me more about Stonehenge," Richard said, turning to make eye contact.

"Like I said, my job was to help set the stones to preserve that location as a way station between planets. When I couldn't return home, I had to first collect enough crystals to sustain the cloaking device for the spacecraft. I waited, hoping my people would return. I had to accept I may have to continue to live on this rock. Once an earthquake erupted and some of the stones were jarred loose. I have a device that levitates the large stones and on one occasion while I was busy with repairs a man stumbled on my actions. He later created this crazy story that I was Merlin and magically moved the mass from one location to its existing spot."

"You have a cloaking device?" Richard picks up a writing tablet and pen from the table, scribbling the facts on the sheet of paper. He soaked up all the information Tom is willing to give him.

"Yes, I managed to move the ship to a cave which I covered with brush," he said, setting his drink on the table.

"So the story about the mass built for Caelus as a Roman temple is not factual?"

"Actually it is humorous since his name is Latin for the Greek (sky god) Uranus." He stood up with his drink in hand and walked over to the fireplace. "I guess in a way if you don't know what's happening, you try to make sense of things."

"Man although not always right will eventually figure out some logical theories," Richard said, as he sips his soda.

"In 1906 Joseph Norman Lockyer supposed an astronomical observation being correct, but no one believed him." Setting his bottle down on the fireplace mantle, "I am eternally appreciative no one listened." A picture of Crystal sitting on her horse hangs on the wall in the study. Tom explores the shape of her face.

"So the placement of the stones is connected to astronomy?" Richard felt glad he had been on the right track all along.

"Yes, they are strategically placed for that purpose."

"What about the stories attached to the God Apollo, medicine and healing of diseases?" Richard tilts his head.

"There is a medicinal element to the circumference." He sipped his drink and said, "If a man would like to call this phenomenon god, I cannot argue with him; this is a miracle of which even I have no answers."

"I have studied Stonehenge myself, especially the acoustic properties and found them more important than everything we have already discussed," Richard said, as he led Tom into his study. "I have cataloged my findings."

"That is the main purpose of the placement of the stones; it sensitizes the sound wave which allows us to bounce off the Sphere and move to another planet." He began opening the drawer of secret information about UFO. "Do you mind if I exam these folders?" Tom said.

Richard walks to the filing cabinet and removes two folders, "I think this may have something to do with your people," offering him the documents. "The crew didn't survive, I am so sorry. We tried everything, but it was too late."

Tom opens the folder. He stumbles to the chair and sits down. Tears form on his eyes and slide down his cheek. He gazes at Richard then back to the open folder. Lifting each page he views the scene. He languishes for thirty minutes without a peep.

Richard left the room and returns with a bottle of Brandy and two glasses. He fills one and places it down in front of Tom. Then he pours himself a shot. Taking a swig, he touches Tom on the shoulder, "I'm sorry."

"Before I carried hope now, nothing." He closes the folder, pushing the sadness away from his view, "The pictures are my mother and father."

"I don't want you thinking like that. If we with our limited knowledge comprehend this much that we also will procure a way to reunite you with your parents."

"They are gone!" Tom said.

"My lovely wife was also gone but with the sphere anything is possible." He walks over to him and Tom stands up. Richard grabs him with both hands one on each of his arms lightly shaking him, "We can do it. Now snap out of this depression and let's get started."

"You're right I have to get a grip."

The noise comes from the kitchen. Kathy and Elizabeth unload the grocery bags. Leaving out the ingredients that will be used for the evening meal. Bert brings in the last sack. Kathy browns the meat in a light season salt and flour with olive oil. Elizabeth cuts up the vegetables starting with the potatoes. Richard strolls into the kitchen.

"We have a guest for dinner," Richard said. "He is the man Crystal called about, I would like you to meet Tom."

"Hi, I am Kathy," she wiped her hand on the towel and gave him a shake.

"I have heard so much about you," Tom said.

"Elizabeth," she said, as she reaches out her hand.

Tom shakes her hand and turns to Bert, "And you are Bert."

"Yes."

"I have lived next door to you for an extremely long time, but under the circumstances I was unable to reveal myself."

"I do recall seeing you before," he glances him up and down.

"I think I should apologize." He rests his hands on the counter, "I monitored you from the airport when you left for Las Vegas. I continued to follow you when you arrived, but you lost me."

"Ha, ha ha," Bert laughed. "You gave us rather a scare, we became concerned that an unscrupulous person discovered our secret."

"Oh, so a piece of the puzzle has been solved," Richard said. A sigh of relief slips from his mouth, "ahh." His eyes go up as though looking heavenward.

"I had to make sure that Richard was telling the truth you know. About being your relative. I had to cover my tracks too."

"I understand my dear boy, you must be so careful," Bert said. "What do you think we start on the new project while the women prepare the feast," he motions for them to enter the study.

"Absolutely," he said, following close behind. Although melancholy about his parents he feels that maybe together they can accomplish more. If Richard beheld his wife again, maybe the same is possible for him and his parents. He shrugged off the depression like a wet blanket and focused on a solution.

Bert should have obtained teaching credentials with his ability to work-out long equations on a chalkboard. He watched in amazement observing the high intelligence. Once Bert finished his theory, Tom ambled over to the scribbled calculations. Picking up the eraser he minus a small section. Adding a new figure. "I think if you move this and add this you will understand the theory."

"By George, I think I comprehend," scratching his forehead, Bert grabs his binder and adds the new calculation.

"I just need to grasp the trajectory of the planet," Tom said.

"That would be Richard's field, hold on I'll get him," Bert dawdles down the hall to fetch him.

Tom stares at the equation and then a slow grin appears on his face, "I got it." He changes one small item and then pulls everything together. He stands back admiring his discovery.

Richard watches from the doorway pausing before he enters observing the new answer. "That's it, that's the clarification we needed to acquire," he said, perceiving what he could only express as an *aha* moment.

"I could not figure the equation myself but when Bert spelled it out for me, well look." Tom's eyes sparkle his cheeks turn rosy as the frown diminishes and turns up into a high chuckle.

"Great, you can explain the formula to us while we eat, the food is ready," Richard put his arm on Tom's shoulder and shepherd's him to the dining table. Guiding him with his chest thrust out. He felt taller, stronger even bigger. Positive thoughts filled his mind. The men had joined together and changed a negative into a positive.

"Did you see the answer Richard," Bert said.

"Yes, do you see what can be accomplished when you work together," Richard said.

Tom felt relaxed whistling an old English tune. He sat in the chair next to Bert. All fear subsided. He really likes Crystal's family and they made him content, slowing his breaths, loosening his limbs. He enjoys the beef stew with every bite.

Each passed the food bowls around talking and sharing the excitement of the found new answers. Cheerfulness fills the room. Tom has a sense of calmness and ease. Richard noticed the change and gives a half-shrug that conveys their secret knowledge. He genuinely likes the young man.

After dinner, Tom accompanies Richard out to the horse stables. Richard picks up a flake of alfalfa placing the food into the horse trough. Ginger whinnies, "hee, hee."

"She seems quite content," Tom said. "How many horses do you have?"

"Oh, I don't have any. Ginger and Shylow are Crystal's," he picks up another flake giving Shylow his meal.

"Your daughter must enjoy them," he said, running his hand along Shylow's ears and patting his face between the eyes. He reaches for the faucet and turns on the water, filling the basin.

"Crystal has always had a dream to raise horses and we are finally in a position to make that come true."

The wild Mustangs gather at the gate and neigh to the horses. Richard carries two flakes over to them. He throws the alfalfa over the front entrance.

"This place is so peaceful," Tom said. He gazes up at the stars.

"Yes, I think this is the most content I have ever been," said Richard, as he smiles.

They amble back to the house. "I will set up a room for you upstairs, we can get started on our new project tomorrow."

He guides Tom up the broad staircase to the second floor. Turning right they head to the bedroom at the end of the top floor. Richard never thought all the rooms would be occupied, a person from another planet above all. He laughed to himself. *If the guys from work could see me now.*

"Here you go Tom. If you need anything; let me know."

Tom said, "Thank you." He reaches his hand up hiding his smile.

Richard closed the door and walked to his room. Kathy reclined soaking in the bathtub. The house is now quieting down. Except for an occasional whinny from the horse stable. Kathy let out the water, wraps a towel around her to dry off. She slips on her nightgown and sashays to the bed.

"I like the young man," Richard said. He removed his clothing and watch. He checked the time, wound the timepiece and placed it on the nightstand. He slips one foot into his jogging pant leg then the other.

"Yes, he seems like a pleasant man." She turns on the light next to her bed, sliding under the blanket, reaching for her book and reading glasses. She places the spectacles on her nose and opens her book. Grins and then removes the glasses, "I don't need these anymore."

"Yes, Tom said, it also stops the aging process." He leans over and kisses her, "Good night."

"Love you," she said, placing her book on the table and turns out the light.

Chapter 18

THE ALARM CLOCK WENT off, Richard jolted awake. He rolled his eyes, spied the time, secretly hoping for a reprieve, but this was not the case. His real life or as he calls it regimented controlled existence must go on. He stepped up to the shower, swinging open the door, turning the knob until he was sure to reach a warm temperature.

"Honey, please tell the guys I'll be home by three. They can get started without me."

"Okay." Kathy wrapped her robe around her, steps into her house slippers, and heads down the stairs. She turns on the kitchen light and brews a pot of coffee. She decided to make bacon, lettuce and tomato sandwiches. Sizzling bacon frying in the pan sends an aroma few can pass up. She pours herself a cup of Java. Places bread in the toaster and removes the plates from the cupboard.

Richard exits his shower and gets dressed. A dark gray suit and matching shiny dress shoes finish his attire. He stands in front of the mirror hardly recognizing his reflection looking back at him. So much has changed since that day in the desert when he found the sphere. Everything happened so fast. Not one person at work even noticed he didn't need to wear the hearing aids anymore. What surprises him the most is how much energy he has.

He made his way down the stairs and out the front door. He strides over to the stables to feed the horses. Once finished he went inside for breakfast.

Everyone is gathered at the table eating. Richard pulled out his chair and slid in. Smiles on the faces could not be missed.

"Sorry I can't stay and enjoy a chalk session with you guys, but I still have to work." He sips his coffee. "I'm sure you can get a lot done without me."

"We will do our best," said Tom. He thought to himself, *I wish I could examine the crashed ship.*

"I will show Tom what we have figured out already, get him up to speed," said Bert.

"Richard, I was thinking. There is a video/audio log box on all the spacecrafts. If you have access to the ship, it is located under the last seat. Most people would miss it. The container is only the size of a cigarette lighter."

"Now that could be helpful. I may even be able to conceal that."

"The mission would be entered and so would the codes," said Tom.

"I will see what I can do." Richard took his coffee cup and his attache case kisses Kathy and waved.

Richard traveled through the halls reaching the debriefing room. He entered and took his seat at the round table. Lieut. Col. Rogers sat across from him. Because the table-top is so large, he felt a great distance from the hostile beady-eyed man, which was fine with him.

"First order of business, you will go to the secret medical facility and receive a shot. Apparently our visitors carried a parasite. The coordinator will also give you enough vials to inoculate your families," said General Harshman.

"Have you contained the organism?" said Rogers, shaking like a frightened puppy.

"We believe so," Harshman said, narrowing his eyes.

"Have you shared this information with the President?" said Richard.

"No, this is a need to know basis."

"Today we will be inspecting the spacecraft. Richard, I want you to go over it with a fine razor eye. See if you can discover anything that will help us figure out its origin," said General Harshman.

"Yes sir," he replied. So many thoughts ran through his mind. Could he find the box? Would Rogers be a problem? Has his family been infected?

"I will assist Clary with the inspection," Rogers said, staring him down.

"No, I want you to do damage control." He placed a folder next to him, "You will need to write a report, keep it simple and confidential."

"But—sir," he sported a flabbergasted appearance on his face, that once again this Clary upstages him.

"No arguing, do as I say," he said, wrinkling his face.

"Yes, sir," Rogers said, staring at the folder, not wanting to make eye contact.

"Now go get your shots and finish this mess."

Rogers looked up at the ceiling, lights glaring down. He shakes his head and his shoulders shrug.

Richard left the room. Closing the door behind him, an imaginary block from the silly man that could not stop fixating on him. Why the preoccupation?

Witkowski has the Jeep gassed up and ready to go. He escorts Richard out. They walk toward the Jeep.

"Did you get vaccinated yet," he asked.

"Yes, sir." He opens the door for him.

Richard sits in the vehicle. Witkowski slides in on the opposite side. They drive to the hospital.

The medical facility is a ten-minute drive from the base, located underground, hidden from the general pubic. Both Clary and Witkowski enter the elevator and make the trek down six floors.

"This place always gives me the creeps," said Witkowski. Stepping off the lift, plowing through the corridor to the hospital room.

"Yea, I'm more concerned about the potential danger of an outbreak," he replied.

The chamber; Richard's nickname for the place, has an uncanny sick smell of alcohol, antibiotics, and bleach. Rita the RN could be seen on more than one occasion slathering the room with the obnoxious product making everyone unnerved. *What was she covering up?* He didn't want to know. Medical supplies labeled and in locked up glass cubbies made a person feel uneasy. White walls, floors and lab coats blind a person upon entering the room.

"Mr. Clary, you must be here for your inoculation," Rita said, as she stares at her clipboard.

"Why don't you sit up here." Running her finger down the list, "Yes, here it is."

He sat on cushioned table, rolled up his sleeve and waited. "Will there be any side effects," he asked.

She pulls out her keys and unlocks a cabinet, "No, this one is stress-free."

Removing a vial from the cold storage, she slips the tip of the needle into the bottle, pulls on the plunger and removes it. Lifting the syringe upright expressing fluid out of the top. She taps the casing making sure there are no air bubbles.

"This will only take a minute," she said, holding his arm, she wraps a rubber element around his limb. She taps his appendage for a vein. One trace pops-up she slides the needle in and releases the fluid into his body.

Richard feels the liquid rush into his arm. He glances down and feels dizzy. He quickly looks away and said, "Is that it?"

"Yes. Before you leave the site, I'll have your kit ready for your family." She lays him back on the table, "Just rest for a minute. I will give you twelve units, keep them refrigerated."

"Twelve?"

"It is just a precaution. The parasite has a nine-month incubation period. General Harshman wants to be on the safe side."

"What, or he may have a baby, ha, ha?" said Witkowski.

"Something like that," she said, tossing the needle into the contaminated control case.

Richard sits up. Makes eye contact with Witkowski and they share an uneasy moment. "Okay, I feel fine."

He steps down from the table unrolls his sleeve, and buttons it up. They march away from the area.

"Did you observe the appearance on her face?" Witkowski said as he guides him to the lift.

"Yea, eerie."

They enter the elevator and thumb the tenth floor. Looking up at the dial as they move deeper underground. The gate opens and they trudge to the spaceship. Richard enters the keycode and lays his finger on the panel. The door unlatches. Once they are inside, he closes the entry.

He pushes the light switch and the spacecraft is exposed. The clean-up crew did an emaculate job. The room felt empty except for their booming voices.

"I'll start on the inside, you check the exterior," Richard said, as he steps into the ship.

He headed for the last seat in the back. Running his fingers underneath the base. He is in luck. The log box is intact. He removes it from the sleeve. Checking all around him before he slides it into his pocket.

Witkowski bounds the perimeter. He spies some symbols on the side of the lunar module. "Hey, Mr. Clary. Come look at this."

Richard steps out of the capsule and ambles over to his side, "Interesting, very interesting." He pulls out his phone and takes snapshots.

"What do you think it says?"

"I don't know. I will have to check our database." He thought to himself, *Tinstelisa.*

"Sir, there is a gap down here by the crushed engine," Witkowski ran his hand through the opening.

Richard snapped a shot and moved back inside inspecting the control panel. He counted the seats and then rested himself in the

Captains chair. He takes a few more photos of the motherboard in front of him. The ships interior seemed mostly intact. After he had clicked several additional pictures, he climbed out of the capsule. One more inspection of the outside and he completed his task.

"What do you think?" Witkowski eyed him.

"I am at a loss," he placed his phone back into his pocket.

They walk back to the entry, shut the lights off, open the door and lock-up the area. They enter the elevator and Richard pushes the knob for the sixth floor. They both glance at the dial. "Do you think the spaceship is from another planet?" said Witkowski.

"Anything is possible at this point."

The lift stops on the sixth floor. They amble to the hospital. The smell hits their nostrils once again. Witkowski's throat burns from the inhalation. He covers his nose and then coughs.

"I can't take much more of this." He removes a handkerchief from his pocket to cover his mouth, he said, "I will wait here."

Richard felt the same way but didn't show it. He entered the room, picked up his kit and signed the release sheet. He spotted Rita with her next victim on the table. His favorite guy; Rogers. He paced back out to the hall.

"Rita has Rogers sprawled out on the table. I think he lost consciousness," Richard said, shaking his head back and forth.

"If I don't get out of here soon, I may do the same." He marched quickly to the elevator.

Richard followed him and entered the lift. By the third floor, Witkowski's pale white face began to show a peachy hue signaling relief. Finally, for what seemed to be an eternity, they stepped out into the fresh air.

They race to the Jeep and make a quick get-away. The Jeep could not go fast enough for them. They arrive back on base and continue their assigned tasks. Witkowski ran errands for Richard. If he needed more documents, he would scout them out. This made the day go by rapidly.

Richard made copies of all the photos and slipped them into his briefcase. By the end of the day, he filed as much of a report that warranted his attention. Done for the diurnal he gathered up the vial kit from the office refrigerator and his attach'e case, which housed the log box, turned off the lights and made his way to the car.

He wondered what information he would be able to gather from the record box. Could he find a way back for Tom? He slid into the car and started the engine. Drove out the gate and ambled onto the highway. Was his family infected? He glanced at the injection kit. One thing was for sure he would have to visit the girls and inoculate both of them. They had spent considerable time with him and he was possibly exposed at the crash site. What he didn't want to do was alarm his family. Tom would also need to receive a shot. The smell of the hospital entered his mind. Honestly the sickest odoriferous ever yielded in that section of the facility, one Richard could not forget.

Chapter 19

ARMS OF CANTERBURY

ELIZABETH TAG NOW EIGHTY years old first earned her 4-year bachelor's degree in biology when she was twenty-two. An aspiring biological scientist she attended classes in mathematics, physics, biology, chemistry and computer science. She moved on to a 2-year graduate program in biological science. Her advanced courses included biochemistry, ecology, neurobiology, molecular and evolution. She also studied cell biology and development. Later she garnished her doctorate at Canterbury Biological College located near Leed's Castle. She has been published for her research experience in "Science and Health Magazine" and Council of Scholars for her "thesis." She became a consultant for government agencies along with a financial grant for independent research.

Although Elizabeth should have retired from her study years ago, she couldn't with the knowledge looming in her head. The night her great son-in-law and great grand-daughter landed on her doorstep; in the middle of the night in 1964. Since time-travel had become a reality, she was sure her exploration should continue. The research lab was moved to her basement of the house in Kent, England. There she conducted her on-going investigation.

Now residing at Lexicon Estate with her grand-daughter and family she knew her choices could only bring success to their challenges. Today she stepped-up to the test.

Richard returned home from a busy day at work. His news sent shivers up Elizabeth's back as he explained the exposure to the parasite and the need for inoculation.

"I will need to save a portion of the antidote so I can replicate the serum," Elizabeth said. She handled the box with care. She moved to the lab with long strides setting the container on his desk. With a slow hand, she lifted the lid and viewed the contents.

He followed her to the room. Tom and Bert, we're still interacting on the chalkboard. Bert scribbled his findings in a spiral notebook. He paused watching the two of them huddle at the desk.

"What do you have there?" said Bert. He lay the papers down and came to her side.

"We might have been exposed to an organism, lovey," she replied. "I will need to give both of you a shot." She searched their judgments for a reply.

"I was informed at the base, we may have been exposed to a parasite that has a nine-month gestation period," Richard said, as he searched their eyes for a response.

"What are the symptoms?" Tom asked. Covering up his body by pulling his jacket tighter around him. He cleared his throat as he slid his hands into the pockets.

"Memory loss, slurred speech and confused behavior. Apparently first the organism attacks the Medulla Oblongata portion of the brain. Breathing becomes shallow, heart rate slows, and then digestion of food stops."

"Oh, blimey, I don't have any of that," Tom said, as he let out the air being apprehended in his lungs.

Elizabeth counted the vials making a mental note of twelve. She slid the needle into the top of the bottle and filled one syringe. She tapped the casing releasing bubbles until it was clear.

Bert held out his arm. She slid the needle into a visible vein and released the fluid. He felt the warmth of the serum spread through his body. She tossed out the hypodermic needle.

Then she prepared her shot. Richard administered the dose. He throws away the remnants into the contaminated waste box. They both turn their attention to Tom.

"Tom, don't worry. I know what I'm doing," Elizabeth said, as she prepared his dose.

Visibly shaking he pulled off his coat, rolled up his sleeve and sat next to the table. "I have to trust someone."

She gave him the inoculation. He sat for awhile deep in thought. He did trust them.

Kathy strolled into the room. "Dinner is ready," she said, staring at the scene. "What are you doing?"

"Honey, I need to give you an inoculation." He sat her down next to Tom.

He explained the whole incident to Kathy while he finished with her dosage.

"I must vaccinate Crystal and Julia, that will leave us with six vials," said Richard. "I will return as soon as possible." He placed two bottles under ice packs and wrapped them, putting the precious cargo in his pocket.

"Richard, I think we should leave three here and I should take the other three to my lab." Elizabeth gazed at Richard for approval and said, "We may need to manufacture more if Tom's people have the infection."

"You are always five steps ahead of me," he replied. Captivated by her intellectual mind.

"Tom, could you take Elizabeth and Bert back to their laboratory?" He glimpsed the approving expression on his face.

"Yes, that would solve two concerns, first making more serum and stop them from aging." He turns in Elizabeth's direction and smiled.

"Richard why didn't you tell us?" said Elizabeth. She eyed Richard for an answer.

"I only learned the truth myself recently," he said and hugged them both. "Now I must get a move on."

He kissed Kathy and grabbed the *Sphere*. They escorted him to the chamber and locked the module.

Richard entered the coordinates of the dorm and quickly transfigured inside their room. Crystal and Julia were prepared to leave for dinner when he arrived.

"Dad, is everything okay?" She embraced him.

"Sort of. But I need to give you girls a shot." He thought to himself, *they don't need to know the whole story.*

"Will it hurt?" said Julia.

"No, it will strengthen your immune system." He rolled up Crystal's sleeve as she sat on the bed, he said, "Which will help protect you against unknown diseases."

Crystal winced as the needle pricked her skin. Then it was over.

He enclosed the plunger and needle into a toxic waste container and loaded the next needle.

Julia rested on the bed with her arm out, not wanting to view the episode in fear of passing out. He finished her injection.

"How is Tom doing?" said Crystal. She didn't want to sound too interested and avoided eye contact.

"He is quite a help which has allowed us to make abundant progress. We will be leaving on a mission when you come home for Christmas vacation." He cleans up the vials placing them into the container and slides them back into his coat.

"Give everyone a hug for me," said Crystal. She kisses him on the cheek.

"I will. See you soon." He patted her head. He set the *Sphere*. The girls left the room and closed the door.

He pushed the pinhole and headed home.

Tom stands out near the horses. He has just finished giving the equine each a flake of alfalfa. Richard opens the hatch and closes the door. He strolls over to Tom.

"It's a doddle," Tom said. He watched Richard step towards him.

"What does that mean?"

"Oh, easy," Tom replied.

"I have to say this is a lifesaver." He ran his hand across Ginger's nose.

"We decided to wait until you returned."

"Good Idea, none of us should be left alone," said Richard.

They enter the house and Richard sat at the dining table and begins to eat the meal Kathy prepared him. Tom sat nearby reading the "Science Magazine."

"How is Crystal getting along?" Tom asked as he kept his peepers glaring into the publication trying to keep nonchalant.

"She asked me the same question about you," Richard said. He plunged his fork into the salad, lifted the mound into his mouth. Picked up his glass of water and swallowed. He is fond of Tom, but now he started to get concerned. What if they enjoyed each other. Richard wasn't ready for an alien/son-in-law. He thought to himself, *how would that work, my daughter living on another planet. Okay, I'm not going to allow my imagination run amuck.*

"I only wondered if she is getting along in her courses," he said, flipping a page.

"Yes, they are going about quite nicely."

Bert and Elizabeth carried a few items in a backpack, opened the refrigerator and added the carton which included the three vials, leaving three behind. Kathy followed them into the kitchen.

"We better get going. I will call you on the blower when we are close to recreating more serum," Elizabeth said. She hugged them and they chaperoned the party to the module.

"I will contact you on the phone at 0-100 hrs," said Richard.

"Have a safe trip," said Kathy.

Tom, Elizabeth, and Bert stepped into the module and Tom set the coordinates. The lights flashed and they disappeared.

Richard and Kathy retired to bed. Both having a sleepless night. Richard overthinking the events. Kathy feeling out of sorts with everyone gone. She snuggled up to him burying her head into his chest. He held her softly in his arms.

"They will be alright." He kissed her on the forehead.

"I know, I just have an overload of information which is keeping the brain active." She lightly brushed her lips against his. Sleep finally came.

Jolted out of a deep sleep by the sounds of horses screaming. Richard stretched out his arm reaching under the bed. He located his Glock and brought the gun to his side. Without turning on the lights, he hushed Kathy by bringing his finger to his lips. He opened the bedroom door and rested his body along the wall as he slid slowly down the stairs. The Lipizzaner kept banging against the stable, but Richard didn't visualize an intruder. He opened the front door and creeped slowly toward the noise. He watched for shadows or any other sign of a trespasser, but none appeared. Ginger laid on the ground inside her stall; wheezing. He peeked inside Shylows shelter and saw him banging his head against the door. *Could they have the parasite?*

He ran back into the house and trudged to the kitchen. Kathy came into the room.

"What is it, Richard?"

"I think they may be infected!" He removed two vials and loaded the serum into both. Kathy followed him out to the scene.

Richard handed her the gun, "Cover me while I give them the injection."

First he entered Ginger's stall and slipped the needle into her neck. He pushed the plunger sending the fluid into her veins. Next he reached for Shylow, who now was laying on the ground. Taking the needle, he inoculated him too. He feared that he may be too late. Now sitting on the earth rubbing Shylow's neck. He raised up and walked back over to Ginger. Rubbing her nose, she peered up at him. The stall grew quiet. Ginger stood up and pushed her nose under his arm causing his hand to wiggle.

A few minutes later Shylow rolled back and forth and then stood up. He strolled over to the partition that separated the horses and reached his head over the railing. His tongue licked Richard's hand.

"That is amazing," said Kathy. She lowered the Glock and a stood closer.

Richard opened the gate and steps out, securing the latch shut. He picked up the needles and they walked back toward the house. "This is more serious than we thought," said Richard.

"I am worried, we only have one vaccine left. If someone else contracts the infection, what will we do?"

"We can only hope that Elizabeth can replicate the serum in time." He entered the house closing the door behind them. He secured the empty plungers along with the needles in the contaminate case and scrubbed his hands clean with bleach. He trudged to the research lab followed by Kathy.

He opened the top drawer of his desk and removed the video/audio log. After hooking up a few connections to the object, an image appears on the screen of his computer. They view the entire mission on the tape. Terrified when they hear the screams of the crew as their mind is tormented by the parasite.

"Tom has been telling us the truth, the team came back for him. I think the man and woman there on the screen are his parents," said Richard as he pointed to the people.

"Richard, I don't think Tom should view their demise." She covered her eyes and put her head down. A tear slid off her cheek landing on the carpet.

"I think we should get some rest. For now I don't plan on showing the footage to him." He unhooked the recording and placed the object in his hand. They turned off the lights and climbed the stairs to the bedroom. Richard tucked the article in his safe. They finally rest their heads on the pillows and slept.

Chapter 20

CRYSTAL REMOVED HER PHYSICS book from her locker and slammed it shut. Julia came along side of her on their continual trip to Professor Morgan's class. They devise a routine right down to flash cards and chronological order of those facts. On many occasions, they received A's on their exams for this diligent effort. They studied evidence from Einstein to Heisenberg and back again.

One thing stayed constant now in Crystal's thoughts *if there is no person viewing the light photons then they have no pattern. But if a person does observe the light photon than it does have a pattern or order.* Crazy as it sounds this is a datum.

Professor Morgan is ecstatic to have two students taking an active interest in his lecture. He would gladly stay after his class to answer questions but until *now* none of his students took advantage of this circumstance. He enjoyed the questioning and even shared his own philosophies.

Julia grilled him on every statement, checking her list for unknown information making sure she has a grasp on what are facts and what she knows are accurate about the theories. She grew more confident as she marked off one by one until there is only a single question left.

"Why do the light photons have a pattern if someone is viewing the experiment?" she asked.

"The only theory I can come up with is the energy in our cells sparks when they are pulled apart. So our energy must affect or create the pattern," he replied.

Julia stared at him for a moment and said, "That must be the answer." She closed her binder after she marked off her last question. They probed his mind for the whole semester and their time together was almost at an end.

Crystal smiled and loaded her book into the pack back. "That makes sense to me."

"Tomorrow is the final exam for the semester," Julia said. She picked her volumes up from the desk.

"See you later Mr. Morgan," said Crystal. She escorted Julia out to the hall.

They left and ambled to the stairs up to the dorm. Crystal opened the door and they rested the backpack and books on the bed.

"Let's go to a movie," Julia said. She brushed her hair and changed her blouse. She wrapped herself in a long length coat.

Crystal removed her shoes and put a pair of warm hiking boots on. She ran the brush through her hair, checked her make-up and reached for her jacket. She giggled.

"What's so funny?"

"We are almost done with this semester and I think I really understand this time-travel stuff more than ever."

Crystal opened the entry and they stepped out into the hall. Jewel cracked the door and peered out.

"Jewel, would you like to go to the show with us?" said Crystal.

"What are you going to see?" she said.

"Starman."

Jewel opened the door wider and grinned, "Sure, let me get my shoes on." She slipped on her snow boots and grabbed her pelt. She stood in the hall and turned the key to lock her door.

They skipped down the stairs and head out of the university. The Boulevard is alive with the sounds of cars and buses as they amble by some bellowing with exhaust. The wind blows lightly as snowflakes drift before their eyes. They enter the walkway to cross the street. The light turns green signaling it is safe to walk. Crystal strides as the other two follow close behind.

The movie theater is on the right just pass the pizza joint. Jewel slips on the wet, slushy snow in front of the cinema but recovers quickly. Crystal opens the door and they make their way out of the cold.

"I would like three tickets for "Starman" please," said Crystal.

The women pull out their money and hand it to her. She gives the bills to the lady and receives three stubs from the agent and distributes out the vouchers.

Crystal sauntered up to the concession stand trailed by Julia and Jewel. "I would like a hot dog, ice tea, and a medium popcorn." She paid for her food and began the task of adding mustard and relish to her hot dog at the array of condiments counter.

Both followed suit each with their own unique concoction. Once they finish dressing their dogs they make their way down the passage to the movie. The theater is already dark as Crystal opens the door and it takes a few seconds for her eyes to adjust to the dimness. Julia bumped into her which causes some of her popcorn to drop from the container.

"Sorry," Julia said. She stops and waits for her to move forward.

Crystal glared back at her then continues advancing. "There are three seats on the top."

"Perfect, I love the highest spot," said Jewel. She trudged in front taking two steps at a time and moved along the row sitting square in the middle of the top.

Crystal slid in next to her placing her armrest down and planting her drink in the hole. "Great seats."

Julia lands next to Crystal. "We made it in time." She takes a large bite out of her hot dog.

The title appears on the screen and moves quickly into an adventure. The room is hushed except for the acting on the screen. Crystal and Julia turn towards each other when they view the first *Sphere* to appear on the screen still silent but share a knowing glare. The drama unfolds and the audience becomes involved with each new insight. Weepy when sad moments transpire and laughing at awkward flashes. Crystal kept eating her popcorn until nothing was left.

Jewel laughed and then said, "This is so far fetched."

"Yes, this could never really occur," Crystal replied. Moving back and forth uneasy in her seat.

Julia knew all too well that the story could happen. Although quite different from their own experience some things made her think someone else must know something about the *Sphere*. The appearance made her nervous and time seemed to move in slow motion.

Crystal kept her eyes fixed on the screen until she decided to glance around the spectators observing their reaction. They seemed in a trance watching the interaction of the actors. Some commented to each other about the special effects.

The movie ended and the lights came on flooding the auditorium. The masses seemed cheerful signaling they enjoyed the show. Only Crystal and Julia wore a stern expression.

They filed out of the hall and made their way out of the theater. Jewel said, "That was a thought-provoking movie, but really the Sphere thing was over the top. That doesn't seem realistic."

Julia tried everything in her arsenal to change the subject. "I think we should get back and study," she said, smiling at Crystal.

"Yes, I need some rest for tomorrow," said Crystal.

"I like the actor, he did a good job," said Jewel.

"Oh look at the time, I still need to do a load of laundry," said Julia. Continuing to walk along the sidewalk.

"What's up with you guys? Did you like it or what?" said Julia.

"Yea, it was good," replied Crystal. She kept her eyes down watching her feet amble across the street. They entered the dorm and moved quickly up the stairs.

"See you tomorrow," said Jewel. She waved and entered her room closing the door behind her.

"Bye," Julia said. She unlocked the entry and shuffled in followed by Crystal.

"Wow, that is so weird," Crystal said. She places her purse on the dresser.

"Yea makes me feel like someone may know more about this *Sphere* or somebody has a big imagination," Julia said. She opened up the closet and pulled out her nightgown.

Crystal lifted her pillow and retrieved her jogging pants. "I'm glad we get to go home tomorrow after our test."

"Me too." Julia removed her make-up and begins to brush her teeth.

Crystal lifted her arms pulling her blouse off and sliding her sweatshirt on. She stepped into her bottoms drawing them up. She walked over to the sink and grabbed her toothbrush applied some paste and vigorously scrubbed her teeth.

"I'll be glad to see my parents," Julia said. She spit out and rinsed her mouth. Taking her toothbrush and placing it into the holder.

Crystal's mouth was full, but she still tried to respond. "Me too." She spit out the toothpaste and picked up her glass to rinse.

Julia sashayed over to her bed lifted her pillow and fluffed the soft feathers for comfort, "Good night."

"Sweet dreams." Crystal turned off the light and wandered to her mattress. She layed down holding the soft headrest close to her. Tom's handsome face popped into her thoughts. His grin had an alluring suggestive shy appeal that she couldn't shake. His laugh deep in a sensual way. The feel of his skin when their hands touched sent shock waves to her inner core. She would lay eyes on him tomorrow and wondered if he would be able to read her thoughts. He must be ancient so this would not work. But he appeared to be her own age. The whole thought petrified her. She was walking on the unknown ground and felt unsure what to do next. Her vulnerability heightened and she felt defenseless against her own feelings.

She found herself deciding what sexy outfit to wear, her red pullover sweater and black jeans. *What in the world is wrong with me?* Crystal concluded to count sheep to get her mind off the striking image in her thoughts. She lastly fell asleep.

He kissed her full on the lips which sent a wave of wild, uncontrollable abandonment of her irrepressible desire. She held him tighter running her fingers through his hair, following the S shape of the curl. Startled by the sensation she woke up. She shakes her head to clear her thoughts. *I have to get some sleep*, she cautioned.

Sleep came again.

Chapter 21

THEY ARRIVE SAFELY AT Tom's home; inside his basement. His coordinates are appropriately calculated for several years, never missing his mark. He was proud of this one fact. He checked his watch setting the new time and announced, "He will be calling in eight hours, let's see what we can accomplish."

"Bert and I will start on the serum and you can prepare the spaceship," said Elizabeth. They both exited the back door and ambled over to their house carrying the vials. Bert removed his keys and unlocked the entry way to his basement. They both entered. Everything seemed to be in its right place. Bert announced he would put on a pot of tea and would return momentarily.

Elizabeth removes the vials from the case and opens up the small ice box placing the containers inside a tube holder already resting on the rack. She cleared the work area making room for her new project. She lit up her research lab and begins removing containers from the shelf over the work area. She lifted her fleece and reached for her lab coat hanging on the hook. Next she put a mask over her nose and mouth and slipped latex gloves on her hands.

Tom carried two cups down the stairs filled with the magic elixir that would aid in their ability to stay the course. He sat them down at a table off to the left. He took a few sips and put his cup back down. Opening the locker, he hung up his coat and put on a long covering that resembled blue nursing scrubs. He too put a mask on and gloves.

Elizabeth walked over to him. She lifted her veil and kissed him lightly on the cheek. Then she gobbled down her tea, placed the cup down, and took a deep breath.

"Shall we begin?" Elizabeth said. Eyebrows raised and a dangerous grin on her mouth.

"Yes, just tell me what to do." His hands raised slightly.

"I would like you to take the test tubes on that shelf and put about 2cc in six of them. Make sure you have your gloves on."

"Ok."

Elizabeth lowered another set of cylinders on her side of the work area. She separated them into two sets. She opened the refrigerator and removed one of the vials. She placed a needle on the top and removed a tiny portion turned to the left and added the serum into both tubes. She took another container and added a diverse potion to one of the vials. Then she made an altered concoction from the ice box and did exactly the same to the other tube.

She began to number each object and documented them in her journal. She added 2cc's to Tom's batch. Then she took four of the samples and put them on the spindle machine. They rotated and three of them turned green. She glared at Tom and began again this time with a new mixture. The new batch turned pink.

She removed her gloves and strolled upstairs making another pot of tea. She filled them each a cup and returned downstairs. She retrieved a bag of sugar cookies from her pouch and smirked at Tom. He wiped his forehead and removed his latex. He extended his hand into the sack grabbing a treat.

Elizabeth started a new batch this time changing up the formula. Once on the spindle one turned red, another black and the last one brown. "I think we may need another pot of tea," she said.

Tom turns the combination on the safe to the right then left and right once more. He heard the latch click and he opens it as the hinge creeks. He removes a crystal and closes the lock; rolling the dial. He climbed the stairs to the food pantry and gathered mostly canned items from the shelf, filling his sack.

He set the location for the spaceship with the *Sphere* and arrives with no incident. He replaces the crystal to keep the cloaking device working and stores the bag of supplies inside the craft. He felt anxious, his tummy rumbling like he is in danger, but he knew it is just his mind playing tricks on him. He needed to calm down, Elizabeth is a biological scientist and he wanted to have faith in her genius. So far not one of them disappointed him. He counted himself fortunate to have crossed paths with the likes of them and now he may even make it home. He checked the monitor of the motherboard, all systems are working correctly. The oxygen levels are a little off. He would need more canisters which he would bring on his next trip. But everything else is a go.

He opened the Sphere and set the course for home. Tom transfigures successfully to his basement. Once home, he trudges out the back door to connect with Elizabeth and Bert but spies a van parked outside behind some bushes. He knocked on the access and Elizabeth answered. He rushed inside and gave her the news that someone is watching the house, but relayed the information with a pad and pen that is on the counter.

Elizabeth locked the door behind him. She wrote back on the pad while she made small talk. "So how are you today?"

"Fine, I was hoping you could come to dinner tonight." He signaled her with a pencil.

"Yes, we would love to come to dinner." She wrote back that she has only to test the serum using a small portion of Bert's blood.

She took a plunger of blood from Bert's arm and dropped three drops in each of the vials. The concoction turned purple and Elizabeth gave Tom the thumbs up sign. She made sure the drapes are closed and began to load all the bottles in the case. Then she packed the supplies she would need in a box.

Bert ran upstairs to answer the phone. "Hello," he said.

"How are things coming along?" Richard asked.

"Fine we will meet you over at Tom's for dinner at 5:00 P.M."

"Okay see you then," Richard said.

"Bye."

Richard stared at the receiver and then hung up. *What is going on there*, he thought. He scanned the phones and the room for listening devices but found nothing.

Bert scampered down the stairs and huddled next to Tom and Elizabeth. Tom pushed the pinhole and the room lit up as they began to transfigure. The back door busted open and two men in dark clothing and masks rushed inside just as they disappeared.

"Dammit, we lost them," said Mark. He waves his gun around the room. He pulled off his mask and gave Walter a protruding glare. "I told you we should move in quicker."

"Sorry, I miss read the situation," Walter replied. His nostrils flared as sweat dripped down his forehead. His gray temples glistened with moisture. His spread out legs planted firmly as though he is anticipating a shootout.

"What am I going to tell MI5 about this?" Mark said as he checked the basement from one end to the other.

"We heard voices," Walter said. Still standing in the same spot.

Mark slinks stealthily up the stairs to the kitchen. Examining the rest of the house. He walked back down the stairs and said, "Someone was here, the kettle is still warm."

"We must find out where the electromagnetic surges are coming from," Walter said, pounding his fist on the wall.

"I can just hear it now, You busted open the basement of a civilian because you detected power surges. They will laugh us out of the bureau," said Mark.

"There was someone here and they were working on something."

"Yea, this is the lab of the biological scientist named Elizabeth Tag, you fool."

"How do you know that?"

"Walter, look at the award on the wall, dummy."

"Oh, shit," he replied.

"Let's get out of here."

Chapter 22

RICHARD GOT ON THE computer and removed any trace of a phone call coming in or out of the Tag residents. Along with any link to him or his phone line. He knew something was up but wasn't sure how to proceed.

"Kathy, I want you to go upstairs and get the gun." He pointed and followed her to the staircase.

She ran up the flight of steps and reached under the bed for the firearm. She grasped the Glock and held it in her shaking hands. She turned and quickly returned to Richard's side.

He reached for the weapon and told her to stay after him. They walked out the front door over to the module. They stood behind the swing of the exit and waited until they were able to make out the figures that exited the unit. Relief rushed over Richard's face when he observed the familiar faces of Tom, Elizabeth, and Bert.

"What the hell happened," he asked. Lowering the gun.

"We had two intruders that busted down our back door of the basement," Bert replied.

"Do you know who they are?" Kathy said. She picked up one of the boxes and helped carry them inside.

"No, but I suspect MI5," Bert said.

"Why?" Richard asked.

"The clothing is standard issue," he said. Bert hobbled toward the house.

Tom followed suit behind the entourage into the front door of the house. He closed the entry. "Elizabeth was able to duplicate the serum."

"That is great!" Richard said. He moved the equipment into the research lab.

Elizabeth opens the refrigerator and pulls out the case. She lifted the lid and stared at the one remaining vial of serum. "Richard why is there only one antidote left?"

He returned to the kitchen and rested his elbows on the counter cradling his chin and said, "We had an issue, the horses showed signs of the infection. I had to inoculate them."

"How are they now?" Elizabeth said. She strolled out to the hall and opened the door. Richard walked up to the side of her.

"They are doing well," he said.

They reached the stable and Elizabeth did a full exam of their condition. "The Lipizzaner's seem fine, but I should run a blood test." She returned to the house and retrieved her medical bag rummaging through her supplies. She let out a deep breath when she grasped the equipment in her digits.

Elizabeth carried the piece of luggage out to the research lab and began setting up her workspace.

Then she removed two syringes and trudged back out to the corral. She stepped inside the stable first taking a sample from Ginger then Shylow.

Richard watched and kept the mare calm during her blood draw. He rubbed Gingers forehead and nose comforting her letting the equine know she was safe.

Next he brushed Shylows back and mane with long slow stroking movements keeping him occupied.

Once the work is complete Elizabeth sashayed back to the practice lab. She placed a dab of blood on the glass slide and covered the dot with the adjoining piece and put the object under the microscope. She lowered her eye to the lens and viewed the sample.

"Richard, I will need more saline solution." Elizabeth glanced in his direction.

"I can get that today in the medical supply room," he replied. Richard left the room and prepared for work.

Tom placed the new antidote in the ice box and moved the rest of the supplies into the research lab.

Bert put the kettle on and made sandwiches. It was going to be a long day. They would sleep in cycles.

Kathy felt inadequate she didn't have a clue how to help. She stood next to Bert as he busily finished making the food.

Richard appeared in the kitchen, he saw the lost look on Kathy's face. "Honey, don't worry, just prepare for the girls to come home. Let us worry about this."

"I wish I could be of more help," she said. Her hands rested in her lap as she sat at the dining table.

He poured himself a cup of coffee, pecked her on the cheek and headed off to work.

Kathy decided to go shopping to get her mind off the whole ordeal. She wanted the family to have a nice Christmas before they started off on their new mission. She wasn't sure what role she would play in their new adventure but is leery of traveling in space after watching the video of the last crew that ventured out into the unknown.

She ambled into the research lab and hugged Elizabeth. "I will be home in a few hours, do you need anything?"

"No, I am fine," said Elizabeth. She picked up one of the test tubes and added it to the spindle.

Kathy grabbed her purse and pulled out her key ring. She marched out the door and got into the car. The Meadow's Mall had new hours for the holiday season. She thought about going there and the Outdoors Man store. Maybe she could help by picking up survival gear.

The traffic bottled up on the highway and she sat in traffic for over an hour. She decided to exit and take the surface roads. She wanted to be of some help for the next mission.

Kathy had many excellent qualities but none that would aid in research of biological antidotes or the curve of a rocket trailing around the earth. She didn't even understand foreign languages or archeology. She has a master's in psychology and taught the courses at the university but became a stay at home mom and housewife two years ago when Richard received a promotion and Kathy found out she had cancer. Her knowledge helped with earthy things like psychology and human nature, or cooking, sewing, and such things. Yes, this did come in handy when they dealt with the serial killer and his victims but how could she be of service now.

The traffic on the main street is clear and she labored on. The Outdoor's Man store is up on the right at the next entrance. She etched on through the parking lot until she spotted an open space. She pulled in and parked. She placed her purse on her shoulder and exited the car securing the lock. The entrance is already crowded with shoppers fighting over gifts. Kathy strolled over to the carts and released one from the train and made her way through the store up each aisle. She decided that canteens could be of use along with camping gear. She wasn't sure what would be needed for the trip but knew it would not hurt to keep these items handy.

This would be a different Christmas. Sure they would have a nice family dinner, turkey, and the trimmings but the gifts would have a different theme than the usual presents from the past. The camouflage clothing sparked her interest. The fabric is durable and most of all they could hide effortlessly. The Coleman stove could work in a pinch.

Then she spotted a shelf filled with maps. She noticed the latitude and longitude markings and felt they would defiantly aid them in the future. She scanned for the ones they did not already have in their arsenal. She placed a compass and flare gun into the cart. Then she was struck by the thought, what if their travel ended badly. She quickly removed the fear and headed for the check-out counter.

The clerk started to enter the items into the register and made the comment, "Going camping?"

"Yea something like that," she said.

The bags loaded and paid for Kathy left the store. Placed the items into the car and scurried out of the parking lot. She traveled to the Alpha Beta and finished her shopping for the Christmas feast. She took the surface roads home.

Elizabeth has finished with the antidote and is downstairs in her room fast asleep.

Tom helped Kathy bring in the groceries and unload them into the cupboard and refrigerator. "Put the turkey in the crisper, I will marinate that tonight," she said.

Tom followed her orders. He said, "Is there anything else I could do?"

"Yes, there are four boxes in the garage marked Christmas, If you could bring them into the living room."

He retrieved the boxes and placed them by the window near the fireplace. He opened one box and shuffled through the items. He never celebrated the holiday but is well aware of the premise. His people always celebrated the winter solstice which he knew stemmed from the shortest day of the year. They could travel from one planet to another after that date, but the best atmosphere is always January sixth. Funny how the planet earth considered the time of epiphany.

Bert hobbled over to the open box. He smiled at Tom and said, "Well we are almost ready."

"I still need to order twenty oxygen tanks," he said. Tom folded the box back shut, and returned to the kitchen.

Kathy finished unpacking the groceries and started a crock pot of chicken stew. She has already added the chicken broth and sliced carrots. The Aroma of freshly baked bread bellowed out from the oven.

She peeled the potatoes and diced them putting the pile slowly into the pot trying not to splash any of the liquid. She lost herself in her cooking. For that moment in time, she was emersed in food. The different shapes and colors livened up a dish, the smell and taste of the unique combinations which brought satisfaction to the taste buds.

Chapter 23

RICHARD ARRIVED AT THE base and started his customary routine. He wrote reports and filed each one. He phoned for a driver and Sgt. Witkowski entered to escort him to the medical facility. They drove to the site and Richard directed him to the storage room. He grabbed a box and exited the facility.

He placed the case in the Jeep and they drove back to the headquarters. He picked up the package and unlocked his car, putting the container inside and locking the vehicle back up.

They return to the office and finish up with the rest of their work. Richard clocked out and drove home.

"I got your saline solution," he said. Carrying the box to the research lab.

"Great, the serum is finished I just need to add the solution," Elizabeth said. "We will have enough to inoculate one-thousand people."

"That should do for a starter," he said.

"I have written out the formula for their biological scientists."

"Dinner smells great, what is she making?" Richard asked. He stood in the doorway.

"Chicken stew and freshly baked bread," she replied.

Richard strolled into the kitchen and lifted the lid taking a spoon that rests on the cutting board and sampled the stew. "Mmmm."

Tom closed the refrigerator door carrying the carton of milk in his right hand. He opened the cabinet and reached for a cup. He rested the glass on the counter and poured the white liquid in. "I need twenty tanks of oxygen for the mission. The levels are slightly off."

"Will we need anything else?" Richard said. He rolled his neck and rounded his shoulders, frowning.

"The craft will only support four, so we need to decide who will be necessary or of help for this expedition," Tom said. He pulled out the chair and sat down.

"Yes, or course you are right." Richard sat across from him.

"Bert should stay here, he is knowledgeable about many things and could be of more help here on the ground. He has a background in the military so he can protect the home front," Tom said.

"Kathy should also stay here, she can keep tabs on the events that happen here while we are away," Richard said. He knew she has completely recovered from her cancer but felt the relief she would be near a hospital and he could focus on the mission.

"I believe Julia may have learned enough to be a help to Bert as far as the time-travel equations and such," Tom said.

"That would leave me, you, Elizabeth and Crystal." Richard rubbed his chin and placed his hand back on the table.

"Yes, I know the direction of our destination, the people, and the spaceships operation," said Tom.

"Elizabeth will be able to share the formula with the techs on the planet and reproduce more if needed and she can be our doctor for the mission. Just in case we have any illness or get hurt." Richard felt confident in her capabilities.

"Yes, and if something happens to me Crystal has enough knowledge about time-travel to be of assistance to you," Tom said.

"Okay, so it is settled, we will discuss the details tonight at dinner," Richard said.

"When will you be leaving to bring them back here?" Tom said.

Richard pushed his suit sleeve on his arm off the watch that rested on his wrist and spied the time. "I should leave now."

"About the oxygen tanks, how long will it take if we ordered them now?"

Richard smiled at Tom and said, "I already keep a supply in the barn around the back. Near the pool."

"You think of everything." Tom shared a knowing grin.

"That's my job."

Kathy entered the kitchen and put her arms around Richard and kissed him on the cheek. "Hi, honey."

His eyes sparkled gazing up at her. "Hi."

"Dinner is almost ready," she said.

"I forgot, Virginia is three hours ahead of us. I better pick them up now," he said. He ran upstairs two steps at a time opened the door to his room and unlocked the safe. He reached inside and grabbed the *Sphere* and buried the object into his pocket, he slammed the safe shut and headed back downstairs.

Kathy waited by the banister until he returned. He hugged her and put his arm around her shoulder. She escorted him out to the module.

Richard opened the ingress and kissed her on the cheek. He closed the door and latched it. Setting the *Sphere* for Crystal's dorm the lights began to flash and then he was gone.

"I think you should call before you come over, Dad." Crystal pulled her blouse over her shoulders.

"Sorry, I'm late. I forgot about the time difference." He turned away while she finished dressing.

Julia walked out of the bathroom carrying her suitcase and said, "Everything is packed."

Crystal opened the safe and tucked the other sphere in her pocket. "I'm ready to go home."

"How did you girls do on the exam?" Richard asked and turned to face them.

Julia handed him the test papers and said, "We passed."

Richard examined the documents turning the pages and gleamed with excitement. "Excellent."

"This question is my favorite," said Julia. She pointed to number five. "About the viewing of light photons."

Richard smiled and said, "Yea, that was always mine too."

They clustered close together and Richard set the *Sphere* for home. The room filled with lights and everything around them faded away until they reached the module.

Kathy was patiently waiting outside the unit. Richard opens the door and they walk out. Kathy embraced Crystal for a few seconds and put her arm around both the girls guiding them into the house. "I missed you, ladies," she commented.

"Me too Mom, and we passed the exam." Crystal carried her suitcase and sat it down near the foot of the stairs.

Julia beamed knowing how much she really is glad to see Kathy. She was like a second mother to her.

The rest of the team busily set the table with plates, bowls, and silverware. The crowd stopped the motion when they entered the kitchen. Each in turn welcoming them home.

Kathy lifted and filled their glasses with apple juice as she made her way around the table.

Crystal carried her bowl to the crockpot and scooped a ladle of chicken stew into her bowl. She cut a piece of the warm bread and sat at the table.

Julia followed suit right behind her. She took the seat to Crystal's right.

Tom pulled the chair out to Crystal's left and glided in. "How have you been?" he said.

Crystal felt the butterflies in her stomach at the sound of his voice. "Fine, I passed the test."

Tom tried not to stare into her sparkling blue eyes but is was no use. He was vulnerable, he knew it.

So did everyone else. Clearly sparks were flying and no one wanted to bridge the subject. Richard most of all.

"Tom has informed me that the ship will only carry four passengers," Richard said. He glanced around the table.

"I wished for everyone to go, but we have a limited space. So Richard, Elizabeth, Crystal and myself will go on this mission."

"Bert will stay and man our return from here and Julia will be his second chair in the event we have difficulty," said Tom.

"Someone has to keep Lexicon Estate running and Kathy knows everything about our home," said Richard.

Richard decided to go into detail about the parasite. He felt uneasy about sharing the information and asked them not to repeat the news to anyone.

Julia sighed. But she understood the dilemma. She knew how important Elizabeth is to the mission. Without her who would administer the antidote or help the other scientists on Alcatisa? "I am happy to help any way possible," she said.

"I do know where everything is and if you are gone Richard, I can hold the fortress down so to speak," said Kathy.

"I do have a military background and I can continue to reproduce more serum. I understand Elizabeth's notes and can maneuver you if something goes wrong," said Bert.

"When will you be leaving?" said Julia.

"The day after Christmas," said Richard.

"I would like to spend Christmas with my parents, but I will return before your departure."

"No problem," he said.

"You can use my car," said Crystal. She went to the counter and opened her purse. She retrieved her keys from the side pocket and gave them to Julia.

"Thanks."

Kathy put some music on and everyone continued to eat. After the meal, Crystal accompanied Julia out to the car.

"You really got it for him," said Julia. She elbowed her on the side.

"You can tell?" she said.

"Yea and he certainly likes you too."

"Really."

"Oh yea, he cannot stop gazing into your eyes."

"Don't do anything I wouldn't do." She grinned, got into the car and waved goodbye.

Crystal sashayed over to the horses. She turned on the faucet and filled the basin. She pets Ginger's nose. *He likes me*, she thought.

She turned off the water and wandered back into the house.

Her mother is hanging up the stockings over the fireplace mantle. Crystal proceeds to take more items out of the box. The Garland will liven up the staircase with the swags of green, beautiful purplish-red bows and white lights strung along the banister. She proceeds to hang the garland along the railing and plugs in the lights.

Now almost a magical winter wonderland and the reflection can be appreciated from the large mirror on the wall behind the flight of stairs. Candles of cinnamon and vanilla are removed from the container and placed on the coffee table and mantle.

Crystal lights the candles and the hall is filled with the aroma. She glanced around the room and made eye contact with Tom. He moved closer to her side removing the gap between them. She could feel the heat radiating from his body and wanted to feel his frame against hers. His lips touching hers. She seemed insane, her mother is in the room; what was she thinking.

Elizabeth and Bert announce they are going to sleep and make their way to the bedroom.

Crystal cleaned up the kitchen, putting the dishes away and the crockpot in the refrigerator.

Kathy and Richard gave her a hug. "See you in the morning," they said.

Crystal sipped on her eggnog and rum and turned on the television. A rerun of "Fame" the movie is playing. Snuggled up in an afghan she watched the program.

Tom carried her suitcase up the flight of steps and placed the luggage in her room. He returned and sat next to her on the couch. "What are you drinking?" he said.

"Rum and eggnog, would you like one?"

"Sure."

"Thank you for carrying my luggage upstairs. That is so heavy."

"No, problem."

Crystal removed the blanket and sashayed to the kitchen. She made him a drink and returned to the sofa, handing him the glass.

She crawled back under the covers and proceeded to continue viewing the program. Every few minutes she gazed his direction. He peeked back at her. Then she did the funniest thing. She lifted the blanket and placed a portion on him.

He smiled and moved closer to her. She giggled.

"Crystal, I want to kiss you," he said, waiting for her reaction.

She turned and grinned, "I want you to kiss me."

He put his arm around her shoulder and pulled her closer to him. He peered into her blue eyes and saw the white speckles light up. He kissed her.

She brushed her fingers through his light brown waves, something she had wanted to do the first time she met him. They held each other close. Their warm bodies aching to explore the unknown secret of passion.

Crystal stood up and ambled over to the television and clicked it off. She returned to his side and took hold of his hand, guiding him up the stairs and entered his bedroom and locked the door behind her.

A wave of heat rushed over her body like a fire raging out of control. She wanted this but felt nervous.

He took in the view of the curves of her body and flooded with burning desire in the pit of his being.

He began to remove her blouse, unbuttoning the buttons one by one until he viewed her flushed flesh burning with anticipation. He took his shirt off and held her close feeling the heat of her body next to his.

She parted her lips stroking his arm holding tightly to him. He grinned and planted his mouth on hers. He laid her down on the bed and rested on top of her.

Crystal could feel the throbbing of his manhood against her secret place and she wanted more. He nibbled her neck and moved up to her earlobes breathing a warm breath that sent shivers up her back and she arched for him.

He trailed his mouth down her neck and caressed her bosom. She moaned with desire.

She gazed into his soul and wanted more. He removed her jeans and then stood up unzipped his, letting them fall to the floor. He stepped out of them and her heart raced.

He climbed back in bed with her and continued his exploration of her secret place until she moaned with ecstasy. He entered her warm, inviting honey pot and thrust deep into her soul until he released his passion for her.

Tom held her in his arms and rested his head on her bosom. He didn't want this moment to end. She parted her lips and kissed him.

"I have to go," she said.

"I know," he replied. He watched her cover herself up with the clothing.

He stood up and walked her to the door. "Good night," he said, kissing her once more.

"Good night." She scurried off to her bedroom.

Chapter 24

RICHARD WOKE EARLY AND loaded the oxygen tanks into the module. He must do an inspection of the spaceship before they embark on the mission. Until now he actually has not been aboard of Tom's craft. He is aware of the location since Tom did map out the area. And Tom did indicate that the capsule is the same model as the one he found near the base. But Richard needed to reassure himself of the safety of the craft.

Tom viewed Richard from the window of his room. He dressed and made his way down to help with the project.

Richard held a clipboard and marked each item with a check mark after loading the supplies into the module. Tom looked over the list. He shivered from the cold morning air. The faint smell of burning wood drifted in the sky.

"I do have four space uniforms on board," he said. He added the suits to the list.

Kathy ambled out to meet them. "I picked up some gifts for the holiday with your trip in mind. I hope they will be useful." She stood and watched them load.

"Thanks, honey," Richard said.

"Crystal and I will pick up a tree. We will be back in an hour." She kissed Richard and walked back to the house.

Kathy knocked on Crystals bedroom door and said, "Are you ready to pick up the tree?"

"Almost, I'll be down in a minute." Crystal finished getting dressed and slipped on her shoes. She thought about last night and a tingle of desire waved through her body. She grabbed her purse and skipped down the stairs to the kitchen. She made a cup of coffee and pulled a banana from the bunch.

"Okay, let's get a move on." Kathy put her purse on her shoulder and marched out the door, followed by Crystal.

They strolled over to the van and Crystal waved to Tom. He smiled and gestured back. Crystal beamed and opened the car door. She slid in and they headed out the gate in search of the perfect tree.

Richard and Tom entered the module and Tom set the coordinates for the spaceship. The lights flash inside the module and then— They disappear. They arrive inside the craft near Stonehenge.

Tom loads the oxygen into the reserve and checks the meter. "Everything is registering accurately on the gauge."

Richard opened the storage room and placed the extra supplies of food into the pantry. He closed the ingress and viewed the oxygen gauge. "Yea, it looks good."

The motherboard lit up when Tom did a power check. "All systems are a go."

Richard stepped out of the capsule and did an entire exam of the ship. "Okay, everything seems to be in order from this end," he said.

They spent about two hours doing an inspection of the spaceship until they are both satisfied.

"Lets head home," Richard said.

Tom set the coordinates and they transfigure back to the module.

Crystal and Kathy are already home and Crystal finished placing the last ornament on the tree when they walked into the house. Kathy plugged in the lights and filled the room with a warm, inviting glow. The scent of freshly cut Noble Fir invited fond memories.

Kathy strolled into the kitchen and cleaned the turkey, placing the spices into the cavity and under the skin to marinate overnight.

Richard walked up behind her and kissed the nook of her neck.

Elizabeth and Bert went into their room and wrapped presents and sipped eggnog. When they finished, they joined the family in the kitchen.

Everyone had leftovers for dinner and enjoyed the tree. Slowly one by one each said their good nights until the house went silent.

Tom opened his door and creeped down the hall to Crystal's room. He entered and slipped into bed next to her. They cuddled and fell asleep. He awoke just before six, put an emerald ring on her finger and scurried back to his room.

By sunrise, the family met in front of the tree. Kathy handed out the gifts. "I know the presents have an unusual theme this year," she laughed.

Each opened their gifts and understood her meaning. For everything would be useful for the trip.

Richard piled the items that would be loaded for the mission in the corner.

"I wish you didn't have to go on this assignment, is it necessary?" Kathy said.

"Yes my darling," he said. "The Sphere summons us again—not to create peace, though peacefulness we want—not to destroy a serial killer though destroying they need be—but a call to unravel the common struggle. Time after time, "happy in capability, proud in troubles, " against a common enemy: a parasite."

The room fell silent as each contemplated his words.

Kathy and Crystal began the duty of preparing the feast.

Tom and Richard stacked the gifts into the module. While Elizabeth counted the vials of serum and made the ice containers for the trip.

By noon, the meal was ready and they gathered at the table. Richard carved the turkey and placed slices on a serving plate.

Tom sat next to Crystal and looked down at her hand. He smiles, *She still has the ring on her finger.* "This stuffing is delicious."

"I made it," Crystal said.

Kathy hoped this would not be the last supper they enjoyed together. Although they have carefully planned for the mission, she still understood the dangers.

"Tom would you like to go for a ride on the horses before we leave?" Crystal said.

"Yes," he said.

They rode out the gate and onto the trail that followed along a shallow river into the canyon. A fresh breeze picked up Crystal's hair and blows around. "Thank you for the emerald ring," she said. Holding up her hand to gaze at the stone.

"I bought that gem when I took a trip to India." He jumped down off the Lipizzaner and walked up to her.

She glided off the horse. He embarrassed her in his arms and kissed her softly. They held each other for awhile not wanting to let go.

"We will have to discuss our relationship with your father," he said, as he glanced into her eyes.

"I know, but I think we should wait until after the mission," she said.

She climbed back up on her horse. He did the same, and they rode back to the estate.

They walked out the horses and removed the riding gear. Shylow and Ginger whinny, as they are placed in the corral.

All the last minute details for the trip are arranged and everyone headed off to bed for a good nights sleep.

Julia rang the doorbell. Crystal let her in. They hugged and exchanged gifts.

"Are you ready for a new adventure?" Julia asked.

"Yes, but I am a little nervous" she replied.

Elizabeth walked past them loading her vials into the module. "Hi, Julia."

"Hi."

One by one they carried the rest off the items for the trip placing them inside the module. When everything was loaded, they lingered there by the entrance.

"I love you, honey," Richard said. He held Kathy and kissed her.

Bert hugged Elizabeth and gave her a kiss. "Keep safe, lovey," he said.

Crystal hugged her mom and Julia. "Don't worry, Dad is a pro."

They stepped into the module closed the door and Tom set the latitude and longitude. The lights flashed and they transfigured.